DOCTOR·WHO

Judgement of the Judoon

DOCTOR·WHO

Judgement
of the
Judoon

COLIN BRAKE

BBC
BOOKS

3 5 7 9 10 8 6 4 2

BBC Books, an imprint of Ebury Publishing
20 Vauxhall Bridge Road,
London SW1V 2SA

BBC Books is part of the Penguin Random House group of companies
whose addresses can be found at global.penguinrandomhouse.com

Penguin
Random House
UK

Doctor Who is a BBC Wales production for BBC One.
Executive Producers: Steven Moffat and Brian Minchin

First published by BBC Books in 2009
Paperback edition published in 2015

www.eburypublishing.co.uk

A CIP catalogue record for this book is available from the British Library

ISBN 9781785940866

Series Consultant: Justin Richards
Project Editor: Steve Tribe
Cover design by Lee Binding © BBC 2009

Printed and bound in Great Britain by Clays Ltd, St Ives PLC

Penguin Random House is committed to a sustainable future for our
business, our readers and our planet. This book is made from Forest
Stewardship Council® certified paper.

MIX
Paper from
responsible sources
FSC
www.fsc.org   FSC® C018179

For my mother,
Vivienne Yvonne Brake (1929–2008)
and for my sister,
Yvonne Lucy Hollis

Trainee Pilot Kareel Rossiter uncrossed her fingers, opened her eyes and let out a sigh of relief. *Made it!*

The hyperspace jump had been perfect: a textbook transition between one location in real space and another, courtesy of a combination of higher mathematics and enough raw power to tear a hole through reality itself. Like an ancient icebreaker, pushing its way through polar ice, the Space Freighter *Tintin* had thrust itself out of its home system, passed through the inter-dimensional maelstrom of hyperspace and then had punched its way back into real space in Quadrant Delta Three Black.

Kareel glanced over at her captain and smiled.

'All systems secure,' she reported, then something unexpected appeared on one of her sensor screens: a small green flash showing another spacecraft. Impossibly, incredibly, another ship had just emerged from hyperspace almost on top of them. Moments later, it was joined by a second spacecraft – the exact twin of the first – and then a third appeared. The relief Kareel had felt after another safe hyperspace jump was evaporating faster than dew on a summer's day. Soon the chunky brick-like freighter was surrounded by a dozen of the alien craft: thin cylindrical rocket ships of an unfamiliar design. The young trainee ran a nervous hand through her short red hair and looked back at Captain Pakola again, unsure what to do. As ever, Pakola, his face set as if carved in coffee-coloured granite, was the epitome of calmness.

'Open a comms channel,' he ordered, as if nothing unusual was happening.

Kareel flicked a switch and nodded at the captain, who leant forward to speak into the microphone built into the arm of his command chair.

'This is Captain Mikai Pakola of the Space Freighter *Tintin* hailing unknown ships,' he stated. 'Please identify yourselves.'

There was no answer.

'Sir?'

Kareel couldn't keep a quaver out of her voice as she struggled to comprehend the story her instruments were telling her.

'Captain, all systems are frozen.'

Instantly Pakola was on his feet and leaning over her station, checking her screens. The data was unmistakable – some external force had managed to take control of the ship's systems.

'There's nothing we can do,' he whispered, patting her on the shoulder. 'Nothing but wait.'

They did not have to wait for long. A metallic clanging announced the attachment of a boarding tunnel, then there was the smell of burning metal, the sound of heavy boots marching and finally, just moments later, the alien intruders were on his bridge. They were powerfully built humanoid creatures, dressed in dark armour, decorated with what appeared to be leather, and huge bulbous helmets. Three of the creatures took up aggressive positions around the bridge, weapons raised. A fourth invader then stepped through the doorway to the bridge, reaching up to release the helmet seal at the neck of his uniform. There was a hiss of escaping gas as the suit depressurised, and then the alien pulled the helmet clear of his head.

The captain remained impassive, but Kareel couldn't help but gasp as the creature's features were revealed: the alien had rugged, wrinkled grey skin, a massive head fronted by a pair of vicious-looking horns – one large one and one more modest – and small but bright eyes. Kareel thought it looked familiar somehow, and then she remembered the Virtual Zoo she'd had when she was growing up and realised what it was about the alien that she recognised; it was almost identical to a rhinoceros, the long-extinct Earth mammal. The alien spoke in a harsh, guttural voice.

'By rule of Galactic Law, this vessel is held in stasis, pending recovery of the criminal agent known as the Invisible Assassin. Your cooperation in this investigation is not required, but interference in our mission will be treated as a criminal act.'

The alien adjusted a control on a device hanging from

his belt. 'You may use your internal communications systems,' he announced.

Kareel was a trainee pilot not a lawyer, but she knew enough about legal matters to know that you didn't argue with Galactic Law Enforcers, and it appeared that Pakola was of a similar mind. Calmly, he ordered his crew to cooperate fully with the boarding party. In reality, they were not required to do much in the way of cooperation; they merely had to stand by while these Galactic policemen searched their ship from top to bottom. The rhino-like creatures were thorough but far from gentle. They virtually took the ship to pieces, stripping panelling from corridors, removing fixed furniture to pull up the floors and ripping out computer units to gain access to service ducts. It was a search so thorough, and one conducted with such vigour, that many vital systems were left completely inoperative. Finally, after three hours of rigorous and methodical searching, the aliens began to withdraw. Their commander returned to the bridge.

'Your manifest shows a passenger who failed to board at your last planetfall. Designation: Aroon Manish. Why is this man not on board?'

Kareel watched her captain swallow hard. She had never seen him quite so unnerved by anything. She didn't blame him for it. There was something inherently oppressive about these huge brutish creatures. Quickly, Pakola checked his log.

'Passenger Manish never appeared at the departure gate,' he explained to the alien.

'What was his final destination?'

'According to his ticket – New Memphis.'

The rhino-headed creature nodded and then turned on his heels and exited. Kareel looked over at the captain and raised her eyebrows. *Was that it?*

'Sounds like they're leaving,' she said hopefully, as the clanking sound of the alien's marching footsteps faded away.

Pakola seemed struck by a sudden thought.

'How did they come on board?' he asked, wide-eyed. Before Kareel could reply, he had his answer as the boarding tunnel disengaged and multiple alarms sounded.

'They didn't connect to an airlock!' screamed Kareel, as her screens flashed red. 'They just cut a hole in the hull!'

Kareel struggled to take in the crisis. Where the aliens had fixed their boarding tunnel, the *Tintin* now had a massive hull breach – a gaping hole nearly two metres in diameter. The captain hurried to her side, and together they started activating the emergency systems.

Thank goodness the aliens removed their stasis field along with the boarding tunnel, thought Kareel.

'Bulkhead doors aren't responding,' Pakola noted tensely. 'I'll just have to try and operate them manually.'

Before Kareel could argue with him, the captain was gone. Left alone on the bridge, she did her best to get other emergency systems under control, but it was almost impossible. The aliens had left the ship in a terrible state. Kareel noticed that life-support systems were failing and, more crucially, oxygen levels were falling rapidly throughout all sectors of the ship. The captain hadn't yet managed to isolate the hull breach. Kareel could feel herself beginning to lose consciousness. With a supreme effort of will, she managed to prime and launch an SOS beacon.

But who is going to answer an SOS out here in deep space, she wondered. The chances of another ship – apart from the alien fleet – even being in the same star system were tiny. Kareel knew, as the darkness enveloped her senses, that she was as good as dead.

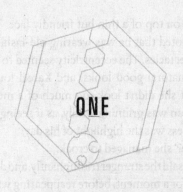

ONE

'Ah, there you are. Welcome back!'

Kareel groaned as she regained consciousness. Her beliefs about any possible afterlife were vague to say the least, but one thing she had been certain of was that death wouldn't be followed by a cheerful voice welcoming you back. She blinked a couple of times and made a renewed attempt to focus. She had a blinding headache and felt nauseous, but somehow she was still alive.

She found that she was looking up at the humanoid face of a complete stranger. From the familiar look of the ceiling above the man's head it was obvious that she was still on board her ship. She really had survived!

'That's it, take it easy,' said the stranger, kindly, noticing her confused expression.

Kareel took a closer look at her rescuer. He appeared to be a human male in his thirties and had a shock of untidy hair on top of a thin but friendly face. The trainee pilot also noted that he was wearing old-fashioned dark-rimmed spectacles. The eccentricity seemed to accentuate the man's natural good looks, and Kareel found herself hoping that she didn't look too much of a mess. For his part, the man was grinning wildly, as if seeing her regain consciousness was the highlight of his day.

'I'm alive?' she managed to croak.

'Oh yes!' said the stranger triumphantly, and disappeared from view for a moment, before reappearing with a cup of water. 'Here, drink this,' he suggested, helping her to sit up and passing her the water.

'Who—' she began to ask, but the stranger interrupted her.

'I'm the Doctor,' he told the recovering pilot. 'I happened to be passing, heard your SOS, thought I'd better check it out, fixed your hull breach, repaired your life support, and here I am.'

The Doctor smiled, slipping his glasses off and pocketing them with one smooth, practised movement. 'Lucky I was passing, eh?'

Having made sure that Kareel was making a good recovery, the Doctor left her and went to attend to the rest of the crew. A few minutes later he returned with a more sombre expression on his face.

'I'm so sorry,' he began, and Kareel could sense from his tone that he genuinely meant his words. 'I did what I could, but your captain was trapped in a section right next to the hull breach. I think it would have been quick…' The Doctor trailed off.

Kareel nodded and sniffed back a sob. 'Captain Pakola,' she said simply. 'He was trying to shut the bulkhead doors, to isolate the hull breach…'

'Tell me exactly what happened,' the Doctor demanded, and Kareel did. As her tale unfolded, the Doctor became more and more agitated. 'Judoon!' he muttered furiously, when Kareel described the intruders.

'You know them?' she asked, surprised.

'Oh yes. All too well,' answered the Doctor airily. 'Great big hulks, clumsy and blinkered. "Justice is swift," that's one of their mottos. Truth is, with the Judoon around, justice is usually brutal and dangerous. They're like the Canadian Mounties – they always get their man. But it's usually at a pretty high price.'

The Doctor looked around the bridge of the freighter, still bathed in emergency red-hued lighting. 'I think they call this collateral damage.'

'Maybe someone should point out the error of their ways to them,' suggested Kareel, not entirely seriously. To her surprise, the Doctor just nodded in agreement.

'Maybe someone should,' the Doctor told her. 'Can't have the Judoon blundering around like rhinos in a restaurant, dispensing justice and causing untold mayhem along the way, can we? Where did you say they were going next?'

'They were looking for this passenger who was heading for New Memphis,' Kareel told him.

'Right then,' he said. 'I'd better get on my way. Before the Judoon cause chaos at the New Memphis spaceport.'

Despite everything, Kareel couldn't help but laugh out loud at that.

The Doctor frowned. 'Did I say something funny?' he asked.

'No, not really. It's just the idea of these Judoon causing chaos at Elvis the King Spaceport, that's all,' explained Kareel. 'As if they didn't already have enough problems!'

Back in the TARDIS, the Doctor fed the coordinates for New Memphis into the destination controls and took a moment to tune in to local newsfeeds to discover what Kareel had been talking about. It didn't take long to find out.

The year was 2487. The Doctor knew that this was an important time in the long saga of humanity's exploration of the universe. At this point in the twenty-fifth century, the human race was well established amongst the stars and had colonies scattered throughout known space. Hyperspace travel had made journeys of incredible distances commonplace, and gigantic spaceport terminals had developed to handle the millions of spacecraft criss-crossing the universe. One such hub of intergalactic travel was Elvis the King Spaceport, a massive construct on an otherwise barren and uninviting planet close to a major hyperspace nexus point, where traffic from a hundred different star systems crossed daily.

The unexceptional planet now known as New Memphis was a typical spaceport. Originally it had been an uninhabited small planetoid of little interest to anyone. Then it had been made the site of a small refuelling base. Slowly the base had become more and more permanent, growing from an automated fuel dump to a fully fledged spaceport. The pace of development had then picked up, and the spaceport had begun to grow in both importance and stature. Physically it grew too, and around it a wider settlement began to emerge. Over the course of a hundred years, the quiet frontier outpost turned into a sprawling city-state – New Memphis – with a permanent population living on and off the trade and traffic that passed through the spaceport.

New Memphis, the city-state surrounding the spaceport, had soon taken on a character of its own. It was a place of extreme contrasts, of glittering haves and downtrodden have-nots, of wealth and glamour, grime and crime.

The spaceport had also continued to develop, but now it found itself having to seek permission from the city it had spawned for every new stage of growth. A plan for a much-needed thirteenth terminal had been discussed and argued over for decades before construction work had finally begun in 2479. Terminal 13 had finally opened just a few days ago, after a long and inglorious development period beset by delays, protests and enquiries.

It was meant to be a state-of-the-art facility that would service both passengers and freight customers with hitherto unheard of levels of efficiency and automation.

It was meant to be the most advanced transit terminal ever constructed, making travel between the stars comfortable, easy and painless.

It was meant to make Elvis the King Spaceport the most popular nexus point for journeys across the sector.

Unfortunately, things had not gone according to plan.

***

'Mr Golightly, it's been seven days now; how long are these "teething problems" of yours going to trouble you?' demanded the pretty blonde journalist. She stepped forward at the end of her question and her floating camera-bot had to adjust focus to catch her intense expression of considered indignation. Standing opposite her, Jase Golightly, General Manager of Elvis the King Spaceport, desperately tried to recall the media training he'd once been forced to undertake and managed to smile back. *Keep smiling, stay calm and use her name*, he repeated to himself. If only he could remember her name.

The journalist, whose name was Stacie Jorrez, waited patiently while he gathered his thoughts, no doubt hoping he would make a fool of himself.

Golightly was a short human in his forties, with thinning hair trimmed tightly to his oval-shaped head. His chubby features were decorated with a pair of old-fashioned steel-rimmed spectacles, a touch of eccentricity that was confirmed by his classic pinstriped suit and the vivid red braces supporting his trousers. Sweating a little despite the aggressive air-conditioning in his office, he pulled at the neck of his shirt.

'Obviously things haven't gone quite as well as we hoped Sallie,' he began, still maintaining the smile, albeit with more than a hint of desperation.

That's a bland understatement, he thought to himself, but aloud he continued on a different tack.

'But then this project has had a lot of bad luck over the years,' he heard himself saying.

Bad luck! There was more to it than bad lack. But where had it all gone wrong? he wondered. *After all the years of planning, how had things gone so spectacularly pear-shaped? And what did that mean anyway? What was a pear? And why were things that were the same shape as pears such bad news?* He realised that he was on the verge of hysteria and tried to pull himself together.

'Bad luck!' repeated Stacie, as if the very idea was an affront to her personally. 'This project has been planned for decades but has been mismanaged at every single stage. It has failed to meet each and every deadline, the costs have spiralled out of control, and delays have become the norm.' She cast an arm in the direction of the arrivals hall behind them and added with heavy irony, 'As passengers have been discovering since you opened a week ago.'

'Well, yes, I am not going to stand here before you and pretend there haven't been… problems, Sallie,' he replied.

Stacie smiled coolly at him. 'It's Stacie, actually.'

Golightly started sweating more profusely and stammered an apology. 'We… we have, er, had some system failures, and, er, baggage complications… software glitches…' he continued lamely.

'But these problems have persisted, Mr Golightly, day after day, with no sign of improvement. I've been talking to some of your customers, some of those travellers who have been inconvenienced by these "systems failures". And they are far from happy.'

Stacie stepped closer again, her body language totally confrontational now.

'Admit it, Mr Golightly, this entire opening has been nothing short of a disaster, a disaster of crisis proportions,' she suggested. The hovering camera-bot switched angles to take a full-screen shot of Golightly, perspiring and desperate.

'I think you're exaggerating slightly,' he managed to reply. 'I mean, it's not as if anyone has died.'

'Cut!'

Within minutes, the woman and her camera-bot had left his office, which was placed high in the administrative block that formed one end of the massive terminal building. Golightly's command centre, as he liked to think of it, had one large multifunctional wall which, at a voice command, could shift from opaque screen to transparent window overlooking the arrivals hall. The wall was currently in window mode, and Golightly rested his head against the cool plastiglass surface and looked out over the crowds below.

He sighed heavily. Despite his bluster with Stacie, he had very little idea how long it might take to get things right. He knew he shouldn't have bowed to the pressure from the board to open when they did, but the investors had poured so much capital into the new terminal that they hadn't been prepared to wait a moment longer to go live. Now they were all facing the consequences but, somehow, it was still *his* problem. He had told them to be patient, to wait, but they had insisted that the declared opening date was to be kept. The media were calling it a shambles and, looking down at the sight below him, Golightly had to agree with their analysis.

The lines were getting out of hand. There were queues at the various spaceliner company enquiry desks, queues at the departure gates, queues at the customs hall, queues at the shops, queues at the food outlets and even queues in the toilets.

Most of the passengers were humans, but there were a number of aliens of various races, not to mention some robots and androids, amongst the crowds as well. Complaining voices, speaking a variety of languages, filled the air from every direction.

Golightly ordered the wall to switch to its opaque state and sat down heavily at his desk. He checked his diary and sighed again. It was time for another meeting with the senior management team, to hear the latest list of problems and the ever-lengthening estimated timescales for putting things right. *Surely something would buck the trend and start to go right for him soon?*

His secretary appeared at the door with an apologetic look on her face. Golightly looked up and sighed when he saw her expression. Whatever it was, this was not going to be good news.

'Mr Salter called,' Miss Fallon told him. 'He said he'll be dropping by for a word before your meeting.'

That was all he needed. Derek Salter was the largest of the private investors in Terminal 13 and the personification of all the pressures to get things right. An unscheduled meeting with Salter was the last thing Golightly needed right now. It had been Salter who had led the charge to open Terminal 13 on the originally announced date rather than accept a delay, and it had subsequently been Salter who had been first in line to blame Golightly for everything that had gone wrong.

Golightly sighed again as the screen slipped from opaque

to newsfeed mode, and he caught sight of himself looking fat, sweaty and rather like a rabbit caught in headlights. 'I mean, it's not as if anyone has died,' he was saying, with a peculiar half-smile.

Golightly hoped those words wouldn't come back to haunt him.

The Doctor skipped around the TARDIS central console, flicking controls and adjusting his approach to New Memphis. Materialising near a busy spaceport was a dangerous exercise, and the Doctor didn't want to be the cause of a multiple pile-up. He needed to make a precise and controlled landing inside one of the terminals itself rather than make any kind of official approach; the TARDIS's lack of pre-authorised flight details would only lead to awkward questions. Thankfully, it appeared that one of the terminals – the newest – had some kind of technical glitch with its security system. With luck – and some skilful steering – the TARDIS could slip in unnoticed and unannounced.

'Terminal 13 it is then,' muttered the Doctor to himself. 'Unlucky for some!'

Deep inside the 'spaceside' section of Terminal 13 a series of connected warehouses contained the automated baggage-handling system that had so completely failed, thus far, to operate according to design. Integral to the system was a security circuit, designed to ensure that all baggage was tracked during its entire journey through the terminal. Like many of the Terminal 13 systems, the security circuit had only operated erratically since going live, occasionally going offline for protracted periods. Unfortunately, as the TARDIS began to materialise in one of the darkest corners of the complex, the system flickered back into life.

Inside the TARDIS, the Doctor shrugged into his long brown coat and headed for the exit. 'Right then,' he said to himself, 'let's sort out these Judoon.' He stepped out and, not for the first time in his many lives, found a hostile reception waiting for him. A squad of security officers had the TARDIS surrounded and were pointing weapons in his direction. The Doctor quickly pulled the TARDIS door shut and locked it before spinning around to face his reception committee.

'Were you expecting me?' he asked, raising his hands.

live, periodically losing Ether for protracted periods of
time. When, finally, the TARDIS began to materialise in one
of the darkest corners of the complex, the system flickered
back into life.

Inside the TARDIS, the Doctor straightened into his long
brown coat and peeked out of the cam. 'Right then,' he said
to himself. 'Let's sort out these Judoon.' He stepped out
and, not for the first time in his timelives, found a hostile
reception waiting for him. A squad of security officers
had the TARDIS surrounded and were pointing weapons
in his direction. The Doctor quickly pulled the TARDIS
door shut and locked it before spinning around to face his
reception committee.

'Were you expecting me?' he asked, raising his hands.

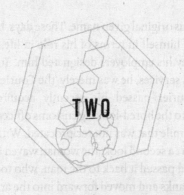

TWO

In the arrivals hall of the troubled Terminal 13 of Elvis the King Spaceport, a traveller destined to go right to the head of Jase Golightly's list of problems had just arrived on a shuttle from Heddon Two. The new arrival was currently shuffling through the slow-moving line of people passing through the customs hall. He looked somehow less concerned about the chaos than most of his fellow travellers. He had one of those faces that are impossible to remember or to describe; a plain, unremarkable face that is instantly forgotten.

According to his passport, his name was Dedrik Gallajer, but that was not a name he had ever answered to before. In the previous forty-eight hours, he had used three different identities – Gallajer, Gorgie Kenrite and Aroon Manish – but none of these was his real name. In fact, the man had so many different identities to choose from that he had all but forgotten his original given name. These days, he preferred to think of himself in terms of his role in life, which was also the way his employers designated him. To those that paid for his services, he was merely 'the Courier'.

The Courier passed his recently acquired identity document to the bored-looking customs officer, giving her a friendly smile that was not reciprocated. Without giving the passport a second look, the woman waved it through a scanner and passed it back to the man, who took it with a grunt of thanks and moved forward into the arrivals hall.

The Courier cast a quick glance at his watch – he was running late. Nevertheless he didn't increase his pace; drawing attention to himself now would be a waste of all his hard work thus far. Anonymity was important to him. He needed to be just another face in the crowd – not special, not remarkable, not memorable. Muttering 'Excuse me' again and again like a mantra, he began to push through the crowds, squeezing between the queuing hordes.

The Courier followed the signs for the left luggage area and made his way there as quickly as he could. He kept a firm grip on his solitary piece of carry-on luggage, a plain grey suitcase on wheels, as he manoeuvred through the crowds and selected a suitable locker. Stowing the suitcase within the locker, the man closed the door and pocketed the reclaim chip. He took another look at his watch and stepped up his pace. Now unburdened by the luggage, he was able to move a little faster. Or at least he might have been able to had it not been for the mass of passengers blocking every path. He began to duck and dive, weaving through the crowd, taking advantage of any sliver of space between people to slip sideways and make progress towards his goal. In the main he managed to do this without making contact with anyone, but once or twice he had a small bump and had to mutter an apology. Occasionally, someone making a similar effort to thread themselves through the masses would collide with him. At one point, a humanoid alien with blue skin had actually managed to knock him off his feet. The alien had been terribly embarrassed. He had helped him to his feet and apologised in a dozen languages as he brushed the Courier down.

'So sorry am I. Please. You not hurt?' he enquired, in a stuttering approximation of human speech.

The man travelling under the name Gallajer pushed the alien's hands away. 'I'm fine, no damage done,' he insisted and continued on his way, quickly blending into the crowd again, just another traveller amongst the masses.

Elsewhere in the terminal, other visitors were making much more of an impact. There were two of them – humans but of such a striking appearance that many would mistake them for aliens. They were abnormally tall, nearly two metres, and dressed in suits so deeply black that they seemed to suck the light out of the air around them. Identical designer shades covered their eyes, and their hair was a brilliant white. To anyone looking at the pair as they strode through the crowds (which parted before them, without being asked), it appeared as though they were the only monochromatic element in a world of colour. They reached a particular café with a terrace area that allowed diners to look out over the arrivals hall and loomed over a pair of Draconians, who quickly finished their drinks and vacated their table.

Across the arrivals hall, the Courier caught a glimpse of the two men and began to sweat. *Why had Uncle sent the Walinski brothers, of all people?* For a moment he hesitated and considered his options. The Courier knew that Uncle was the big noise in the criminal underground of New Memphis, but he also knew that there was a new gang in town, an upstart criminal organisation run by the mysterious Madame Yilonda. His job was to take items from one place to another and not to ask too many questions about what he was carrying or why. Right now, he was meant to be handing over the reclaim chip to the agents Uncle had sent to the rendezvous point, and if those agents happened to be the Walinski brothers then Uncle must have his reasons. As far as the Courier was concerned, sending the Walinski brothers was akin to putting a huge spotlight on his arrival and calling up Madame Yilonda directly to tell her to take a closer look. It was a worrying thought. *Why arrange for something to be delivered from off-world with such secrecy and then make such a public showing of making the collection?* Something didn't smell right, and the Courier was very tempted to cut and run.

The Walinski brothers were more than just albino freaks, though. The Courier knew their reputation well. They were Uncle's most trusted enforcers; cross Uncle, and the Walinski brothers would travel the length of the universe to track you down. Cutting and running was just not an option.

***

'You can lower the weapons, you know,' the Doctor told the security men brightly. 'I'm not about to do a runner.'

There were four security officers in the squad, all dressed in smart, matching uniforms with polished boots and shiny weapons. They looked young, keen and, perhaps, just a little bit nervous. Beyond their original instruction to the Doctor to raise his hands, they had not said a word. The Doctor guessed they were waiting for someone with more authority to arrive and take charge.

A moment later, a man in a similar but slightly grander uniform appeared in a distant doorway and began marching towards them. As he approached, the Doctor could see that he was significantly older than his officers. His lined and scarred face, coupled with his gait, told the Doctor all he needed to know. Ex-military, he decided.

'Transit documents?' demanded the man before he had even reached the group.

One of the young security guards shook his head.

The older man came to a halt directly in front of the Doctor and subjected him to an intensive visual appraisal.

'You realise that this is a secure area of the spaceport?' he asked eventually, maintaining eye contact as he spoke.

The Doctor nodded and pulled his psychic paper from his jacket pocket, leaning forward to whisper in the man's ear. 'Undercover agent, Galactic Law Authority,' he told him. Without replying, the ex-soldier took the wallet and gave it a long cool look before handing it back.

'Looks like a blank sheet of paper,' he retorted. 'Don't try any of your psychic mind games on me, sonny, not to a veteran of the Telepath Uprising of '54.'

The Doctor quickly slipped the wallet back into his pocket and changed tack without missing a beat.

'Veteran of the Uprising, eh? I should have guessed. If they've called someone of your standing in here, things must be worse than I thought.'

The ex-soldier nodded to two of the guards who moved in and twisted the Doctor's arms behind his back.

'And don't think you can flatter me, either,' he told the Doctor, turning his back on him. 'This way please.' The man began marching off in the direction from which he had come. The Doctor found himself manhandled along in his wake by two of the fresh-faced security men.

As they walked, one of the guards gave the Doctor a sympathetic look before hurrying off after his commanding officer.

'Upsetting General Moret was a really bad idea,' he told the Doctor in a whisper as he passed him.

Considering the way things had gone, the Doctor had to agree with the analysis. Things were not looking good.

The Courier swallowed hard as he sat down at the table with the Walinski brothers. Three steaming cups of coffee were waiting on the table, but something still felt odd, something didn't look quite right. *Was there something unusual about the bubbling liquid in the cup in front of him or was he just being paranoid?*

'Surprised to see you boys on this errand – what happened, did one of you do something to upset Uncle?' he asked, realising that he sounded a little nervous. *How could he let the Walinski brothers get to him like this – where was his professionalism?* The brothers treated the question as if it was rhetorical and said nothing. The Courier glanced down at the coffee cup in front of him. It was still bubbling suspiciously. *Better safe than sorry.* He moved the cup and swapped it with one of the brothers' drinks.

'Not that I don't trust you or anything... but, well, I don't!' he explained.

To his surprise both brothers just grinned at this and, in perfect synchronisation, they slipped their dark glasses up onto their foreheads. Two pairs of pink eyes now looked directly at him.

'No offence meant...' said one brother.

'No offence taken...' concluded the other, completing the sentence as if the two were part of the same consciousness.

The two continued to look at him, their expressions as illegible as a medic's handwriting. The Courier picked up the cup of coffee and raised it to his lips. He hesitated for a beat and then, under the intimidating eyes of the brothers, he took a sip. He was relieved to find that it tasted completely normal.

'Is the "package" secure?' asked the first brother, with the same casual tone that one might use to discuss the weather.

The Courier took another sip of his coffee before answering.

'Left luggage,' he said simply, replacing the cup on the table.

The Walinski brother on his left held out a hand.

'Reclaim chip?'

The Courier noted with surprise that he was sweating. Either the Walinski brothers were getting to him or the coffee had been hotter than he had realised. He reached into his pocket and felt a sharp stabbing in his stomach – the chip wasn't there. Quickly he checked his other pockets. He was sweating profusely now, heartbeat racing – *how was this possible? He had pocketed the chip just minutes ago.*

Both brothers kept looking at him with intense expressions. It was as if they were both heat sources pouring down on him. Sweat was now running off him as if he were in a sauna. His clothes were drenched, his hair sodden. Carefully, methodically, he checked each and every pocket of his clothing. The chip was nowhere to be found.

'I had it a moment ago,' he told them desperately, but they seemed to have lost patience with him. They exchanged a look and a nod then abruptly pushed back from the table and stood up. Without looking back at the Courier, they quickly moved away from the café and disappeared into the crowd.

The Courier didn't know what to do. When the Walinski brothers reported this failure to Uncle, he would be as good as dead. *Unless, somehow, he could turn this around and make good on his error. What could have happened to that chip? It had been safe in his pocket and now it was gone… Of course!* Suddenly he remembered the blue-skinned alien who had run into him. What a fool he had been; it was a classic pickpocket technique. The thief would 'accidentally' run into their mark and then, under cover of helping the victim to their feet, they would stealthily pick their pockets.

The Courier realised that his only hope of surviving was to find the pickpocket and get that chip back. He got up and was surprised to find that he was unsteady on his feet. He swayed, his head spinning. He was still sweating profusely, unnaturally. All in all, he felt quite unwell.

Pushing himself away from the table, he staggered to the nearest washroom. He almost fell through the doors and stumbled across to the washbasins. People were avoiding him now, unnerved by the sight of a man sweating and shivering so badly. He realised that he must look quite ill to people, perhaps even dangerous. He looked up at his reflection in the mirror above the sink and was horrified at the sight that met his eyes. His skin was actually glowing – changing colour from a burnt orange to a deep blood-red even as he watched. He looked like he'd been exposed to some kind of terrible radiation source. He jerked the tap on and splashed cold water onto his face. It hissed, instantly turning to steam as it touched his overheating skin. Flailing now, he splashed more and more water upwards onto his person but it wasn't enough. He could feel himself getting hotter and hotter, brighter and brighter.

Suddenly his clothes burst into flame, and seconds later his entire body was engulfed with fire. For a moment he burned with the intensity of an inferno and then – with a deafening bang – he exploded.

The Doctor and his captors had just emerged into the public area of Terminal 13 when the reports came in on the security guards' radios. The screams and cries of panicking travellers had already alerted them to the fact that some kind of incident had occurred but, with the mass of people in the arrivals hall, it was not possible to determine the exact site of the problem just by looking.

General Moret turned to the Doctor. 'We need to attend to an emergency. You will accompany us. Make any move to escape and my men will shoot you without warning. Understood?'

'Crystal clear,' the Doctor replied.

The General looked at him for a moment, then seemed to make a decision to trust the stranger and started leading the squad towards the incident.

'Suspicious death of a passenger,' he told the squad as they moved. Moments later they reached the public toilets where the Courier had met his fate. There was a smell in the air, reminiscent of barbecues, and the Doctor realised with some horror that it was the smell of burnt flesh. The Doctor watched, fascinated, as the General took charge, deploying his men to deal with the public and directing the other emergency services when they arrived on the scene. Some cosmetic damage to the fixtures and furnishings had been caused by the exploding man, but the intense heat had mostly been contained by automatic fire-suppressant systems.

'At least something works round here,' muttered the young security officer who had spoken to the Doctor earlier. The badge on his uniform gave his name as Adams. He had been assigned the task of keeping an eye on the prisoner while the incident was dealt with.

'Things not been going too well?' the Doctor asked him.

'You can say that again,' replied Adams with feeling. 'This whole terminal has been a disaster. Looks like the Chief's getting the gen on what happened here.'

On the far side of the room, a specialist medical team was carefully collecting what little remained of the victim and placing it on a gurney.

The Doctor and Adams watched as General Moret thanked the attending physician and walked back to rejoin them.

'Spontaneous human combustion,' Moret announced as he reached them. Behind him, the paramedics began manoeuvring the gurney out of the room.

'I doubt it,' commented the Doctor quietly.

The General turned and gave him a suspicious look. 'Know something we don't, do you?' he demanded.

The Doctor shook his head. 'Not about this case, no. But I know a little about so-called spontaneous human combustion.'

'Would you care to share your knowledge?' asked the security man with more than a hint of sarcasm, an undertone the Doctor chose to ignore.

'Well, for a start, "spontaneous" is completely wrong. Human flesh can burn but not spontaneously; it needs something to make it happen.'

'So are you saying this is a murder?' asked a new voice.

The Doctor turned to see a slightly overweight man in a suit entering the room, the security cordon parting for him without any hesitation.

Adams leant forward and whispered in the Doctor's ear. 'Mr Golightly, General Manager of the spaceport.'

The Doctor reached out and shook Golightly's hand, taking him by surprise.

'It is a murder, I'm afraid, sir. And a rather nasty one at that.' The Doctor flashed him one of his most confident smiles. 'You'll be glad I'm here.'

General Moret narrowed his eyes. 'This man is a prisoner. He was in a secure area without authorisation,' he told Golightly urgently.

The Doctor put an arm around Golightly's shoulder and turned him away from the General.

'All a bit of a misunderstanding,' he whispered. 'I'm sure I can explain…' He reached inside his pocket for the wallet containing his psychic paper.

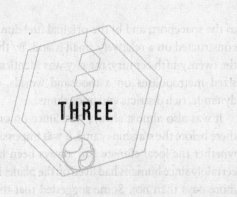

THREE

Outside the gleaming halls of the spaceport, the city-state of New Memphis was a much less glamorous environment. A recent edition of *1001 Galactic Destinations to Die Before You See* had listed it in its top ten places to do anything to avoid visiting. In its review, the book had referred to its dated, functional architecture, the unfriendliness of its natives and the rampant crime levels that made New Memphis a haven for undesirables from across ten sectors.

The book's summary wasn't an exaggeration. New Memphis was a sprawling urban mess, unplanned and frequently unregulated in its rapid growth. It had begun with living areas close to the spaceport borders and had spread like a rash from there: a mixture of retail, commercial and residential buildings, packed tightly into a tiny footprint of land because a) everything revolved around rapid access to the spaceport, and b) the original fuel dump had been constructed on a relatively small island. By the middle of the twenty-fifth century, the city was identical to similar-sized metropolises on a thousand worlds, diverse and dynamic, rich districts and poor slums.

It was also almost always wet. Since no one had lived there before the starships came, it was impossible to know whether the local climate had always been like this, but certainly since humans had lived on the planet it had rained more days than not. Some suggested that the persistent rain was a reaction to the pollution caused by the massive spacecraft pouring in and out of the many Elvis the King terminals but it was a moot point as nobody was going to suggest anything that might limit the traffic in any way – the spaceport was too important to the local economy.

Just as vital to the city-state was the criminal activity. As in many frontier settlements, law was an optional element in New Memphis society and the various criminal gangs and crime lords were as important as, if not more important than, the elected officials in shaping day to day life in the city.

That's not to say that there were no law-abiding citizens in New Memphis. Just that they were not necessarily the majority.

In one of the city's less salubrious districts lay the distinctly downmarket Hound Dog Shopping Mall. When it had first been built, it had been one of the grandest retail developments in the sector, full of fashionable boutiques. Now it was a rather sad shadow of its former self, with numerous units lying empty and many of the others given over to tatty stores selling factory rejects and seconds. In the Blue Hawaii Food Court, a few desperate souls were risking life and limb eating poorly cooked Kronkburgers and limp fries.

Most of the staff looked as lifeless as the food they were serving, but one waitress seemed more alive than all the rest put together. She was a pretty, blonde-haired teenager, who managed to make the shapeless blue uniform look vaguely attractive as she bustled between the tables, bestowing a cheerful smile on the undeserving punters and generally single-handedly raising the mood in the place.

The owner of the Food Court, a rat-faced man by the name of Sten, looked on with satisfaction as the new girl, Nikki, delivered a pair of Giant Kronkburgers to a couple of young men who had squeezed into a booth at the very back of the eating area. Hiring Nikki had been a really good move. Sten couldn't believe his luck. She was both prettier and brighter than anyone he'd employed before.

Nikki carefully placed the plates of food in front of the two men and waited. Neither of the customers even glanced in her direction but continued to talk in hushed tones, as they had done since they had arrived twenty minutes earlier. Making sure they were still absorbed in their conversation, she reached under the table to check that the device she had put there when taking their order was still in place. Her fingers ran over the tiny bug and confirmed that the unit was working properly. Every detail of the men's intimate chat would be transmitted across to the unit's base which she had left under the counter and recorded for posterity.

Suddenly one of the men looked up at her.

'Do you mind? This is a private conversation,' he hissed.

Nikki put on a good act of being surprised.

'What? Oh sorry I was miles away. Can I get you gentlemen anything. Relish, mustard, green sauce?' Nikki deliberately made her voice higher-pitched than normal, which immediately took a few years off her and made her sound almost childish.

'No, nothing,' replied the man, rudely.

'No worries,' said Nikki perkily. 'If you need anything I'll be right over there.'

Nikki hurried back to the counter and checked the other end of the bug. Perfect! Everything the men were saying was coming through loud and clear and getting captured on the unit's memory.

Now if they'd just say something incriminating, her job – her real job – would be done.

Nikki Jupiter might have looked the part of a Blue Hawaiian waitress but she was, in fact, something very different.

Nikki Jupiter, at just seventeen, was a very accomplished private detective.

General Moret was not impressed. Golightly had ignored his protests about the validity of the stranger's credentials, and seemed to have accepted the Doctor completely. Moret had been ordered to release the Doctor and to cooperate fully with both the stranger and the local authorities in the investigation of the incident. General Moret was far from happy with this turn of events, but he had no choice: Golightly paid his wages. Not for the first time since his retirement from his first career, Moret longed for the old days. Life as a Space Marine had been so simple compared to this security lark.

The Doctor was being briefed by Jase Golightly who was telling him the whole sorry saga of Terminal 13. The Doctor interrupted him to ask if he'd had any contact from Galactic Law Enforcers. Golightly shook his head.

The Doctor pulled a face. 'Then I'm very sorry, but I think you're about to.'

'I thought you were—' began Golightly.

'Plainclothes,' interrupted the Doctor quickly. 'Well not so much plainclothes as freelance, local expert, that kind of thing. It's the beat coppers with their size twelves you need to worry about.'

Golightly shook his head, not really understanding. 'I need to get back to the office. I have to keep a lid on this thing. Missing luggage and travel delays are one thing; passengers exploding on their way through the terminal is something else again.'

'There were plenty of witnesses,' commented the security chief.

Golightly stopped, realising the truth of Moret's statement. He thought desperately for a moment.

'Find them. Offer them free flights, whatever it takes. I don't want this story getting out. Not to the newsfeeds and not to the board either.' Golightly shivered, remembering that Derek Salter was on his way in to see him. If Salter got to hear about this… It wasn't worth thinking about.

Golightly's bad day wasn't over yet. There was a sudden and enormous sonic boom, and all the lights went out. Moments later, emergency lighting came on, casting an eerie blue glow over everything. Then came the sound – a regular rhythm of thudding feet, leather boots on metal walkways, getting louder and closer.

Golightly followed the noise, emerging from the washroom into the arrivals hall where the crowds were parting to let through a column of armoured creatures. Golightly had no idea whose army this was but knew it was bad news.

As he left, General Moret bristled; he recognised military marching when he saw it and these were clearly well-drilled troops. He hoped they were not hostile.

The Doctor, alone amongst the group, not only knew exactly who the strangers were but had been expecting them. 'The Galactic Law Enforcement officers I told you about,' he whispered to Golightly. 'Judoon.'

Golightly took at step or two forward to intercept the incoming law enforcers as the Judoon came to a halt.

'Jase Golightly, General Manager of this facility,' he introduced himself.

The lead Judoon inclined his head to look down at the human addressing him. For a long moment he seemed to be considering his next move, and then he removed his helmet revealing his rhino's head.

'This terminal is under Judoon lockdown,' the Judoon Commander announced. 'No one will be permitted to leave or enter until our search is complete. Cooperation is required. Under Galactic Law Statute Forty-Three, all life forms in this facility will present themselves for identity verification and a personal search.' He paused for a moment to allow his words to sink in. 'All areas of this terminal are to be made available for a complete search.'

'Going to leave this place in the same state as the *Tintin* are you?' wondered the Doctor.

The Judoon Commander turned to glare at the Doctor. 'Identify yourself,' he ordered.

'I'm the Doctor. I happened to be passing and saved the crew of the *Tintin* after you left it all but crippled,' explained the Doctor.

'Justice must be served,' the Judoon responded. 'It was not our intention to render the freighter inoperable.'

'It might not have been your intention, but it was the result,' retorted the Doctor angrily.

The Judoon stared down at the smaller figure. 'The search will begin immediately. No unnecessary damage will be caused.'

'The search for what?' asked the Doctor.

'The Invisible Assassin,' replied the Judoon simply.

With that the Judoon Commander turned away and started to dispatch his Judoon warriors to their various tasks in the search.

The Doctor stepped up to stand beside Golightly. The man was shaking, though whether from fear or anger it was hard to say.

'Well, at least I tried. Let's hope they find what they're looking for quickly.'

'Are these your coppers with size twelve boots?' wondered Golightly.

The Doctor nodded. 'Big, brutal and clumsy. Just what you don't need in a police force.'

Nikki was busy wiping down the counter. Or at least that was what she wanted people to think she was doing. She was actually concentrating on the conversation going on in the rear booth. The two men were still talking, spilling useful information about the gang they were involved with – the upstart criminal organisation known as the Widow's Gang. More specifically, they had just confirmed their personal involvement in the case Nikki was most interested in. There had been a jewellery heist last month, but the police had swiftly come to the conclusion that there was a lack of credible evidence to follow up and had closed the file after just a day's work. The shop owner, unhappy with the service, had come to the Jupiter Detective Agency to see if they could succeed where the police had failed. Nikki had been manning the office, as she often did when her father was out on a case, and when he returned that night she'd asked if she could take the jewellery investigation herself. Her dad, of course, had said yes. He never could say no to his little girl.

Thinking of her father brought Nikki up short for a moment and she lost focus on the job at hand. *Where was he?* It had been three weeks now since he'd gone off to do a job somewhere in the spaceport. It wasn't the first time he'd been away, but he normally managed to keep in touch a little better than this. In twenty-one days she'd had a couple of e-mails and one phone message, all of such brevity that they hardly counted as contact at all. What was really strange was that he'd said nothing about the case he was working. Normally he shared everything with her. She didn't want to be negative or think the worst but she knew a private detective's life was a dangerous one. People were never very happy to be snooped on.

Suddenly she snapped out of her reverie. Something was happening at the table that she was meant to be watching. The voices in her earpiece had stopped and when she looked across to the seating area she could only see one of the men. Then the other appeared, clutching a fork in one hand. He must have dropped it and ducked under the table to find it. Nikki's heart jumped in her chest. *What if he'd found the bug?* Too late! Nikki could see that he was showing something to his friend, who now jumped to his feet, looking around in a paranoid fashion. His eyes locked with hers, and she knew instantly that her cover was blown.

The man who had found her little toy was already running for the exit but the second man was reacting more aggressively. Standing clear of the table, he reached into his coat pocket and produced a stubby-looking hand weapon.

Diving for cover would have been one option but, without knowing exactly what the weapon could do, offence was a better strategy than defence. Nikki vaulted the counter and ran directly towards the armed man. In what seemed to be slow motion, he continued to bring the weapon up and aim it directly at her, but Nikki was no longer on her feet. Using a table to launch from, she planted her hands, jumped and twisted in the air, kicking the weapon out of the slack-jawed gunman's hand. She landed like a gymnast, spun, hit out with a martial arts punch then spun again, this time on one leg, and felled the man with a sharp kick to the head. The entire fight had taken about five seconds, but that had been enough to give the first man a good head start.

Nikki immediately gave chase. The evidence she had gathered would be useless if the guy escaped. The Widow's Gang would make sure he disappeared for a while if necessary; the only way to get justice for her client and recover some of the stolen jewellery was to capture the bloke now.

Skidding out into the main corridor, she looked both ways. Luckily the mall was not very full and she quickly spotted her quarry running towards the north exit. She set off in pursuit, her long legs propelling her rapidly after the man. Shoppers, seeing the girl running towards them so purposefully, jumped to get out of her way. Ahead of her, the man carried on but he appeared to be slowing – perhaps the Giant Kronkburger was doing her a favour.

Nikki pounded on. The man looked back over his shoulder and saw how close his pursuer was. Suddenly he jerked to the left and ducked into a clothes shop. The store was full of racks of factory seconds, making it an untidy maze. When Nikki reached the door she paused, unable to see her quarry.

Suddenly an entire rack of clothing started tipping towards her. She jumped back and managed to get clear of the falling rack. As it clattered to the floor, it revealed her target behind it. Not hesitating, Nikki vaulted over the scattered clothes and advanced on the man, who looked around desperately for a weapon or some cover. Neither were on offer.

Nikki set herself in a martial arts stance: arms raised ready, knees bent. The man responded by turning to run, but only succeeded in getting his feet caught up in some of the spilt clothing. He flew through the air and clattered into a display of shop dummies. Falling to the floor heavily, he stayed down. Nikki pulled out her phone and called the police.

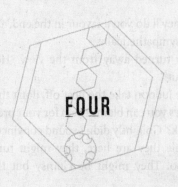

FOUR

Jase Golightly stood at the wall-length window overlooking the arrivals hall and winced. Below him, the usual chaos of the past few days had been replaced by something far worse.

The Judoon had poured into the terminal in massive numbers and had begun processing all the passengers. One by one, each individual was identity-checked and searched and, once cleared, they were sent out of the terminal into the wider spaceport beyond.

Elsewhere, even more Judoon were searching every square centimetre of the complex, both public and 'backstage' areas. Despite the Doctor's words of warning, the Judoon didn't seem to be taking any more care than normal about their work. Displaying the same carelessness that had almost destroyed the *Tintin*, they were now taking apart the not-long completed new Terminal 13.

'Maybe they'll do you a favour in the end,' commented the Doctor sympathetically.

Golightly turned away from the view. 'How do you make that out?'

'Well, the Judoon take the heat off, don't they? For the next few days you can blame them for your problems.'

'You think?' Golightly didn't sound convinced.

'And while they are here, they might turn up your gremlins too. They might be clumsy but they're very thorough.'

'You think this "Invisible Assassin" that they're looking for is connected to the missing luggage?' Golightly asked.

The Doctor shrugged. 'I don't know. But I'd like to find out.'

Golightly looked at him carefully. 'Can you help? You seem to know these Judoon…'

'Tell me more about what's been happening,' the Doctor suggested. 'Perhaps I can see a pattern you've missed.'

Golightly wandered across to the desk and sat down in his chair. 'You know about the troubled path we had to travel to even get Terminal 13 open?'

'Oh, don't tell me – public enquiries, protests, planning problems…?'

Golightly nodded. 'Every delay you can imagine, and then some more. But finally we got the go-ahead and construction began.'

The Doctor had now moved across to the window and was looking down on the Judoon activity below. 'But the problems continued?'

'No more than any other major construction project, I

suppose. But it felt endless. And then there was the rush to open. The investors insisted that we open on the day we originally announced. We weren't ready. But they wouldn't listen to reason.'

'To be fair,' interrupted a new voice, 'it was me that insisted.'

The Doctor turned to see that a man in an old-fashioned wheelchair was propelling himself into the room. The new arrival was in his fifties, tanned and healthy looking despite the wheelchair. He rolled himself over to the Doctor and extended a hand.

'Derek Salter,' he introduced himself. 'I own sixty per cent of this terminal.'

The Doctor took his hand and noted that Salter was one of those men who used a handshake to make a point – he felt Salter's hand enclose his own and squeeze firmly while maintaining eye contact. 'So don't let anyone kid you. I was the one responsible. It was me that insisted we open on time, so I'm the one with egg on my face,' he explained, finally releasing the Doctor's hand.

'Anyone can make a mistake,' muttered the Doctor, trying to rub some life back into his bruised hand.

'Mistakes cost money. More to the point *this* mistake is costing me money.' Salter slammed his hand down on the armrest of his chair for emphasis. 'I need this terminal to be fully operational and a roaring success. That's the bottom line. Literally.'

Salter spun around to face Golightly.

'So what progress have you made? Has anyone found all this lost luggage? And what about the software glitches?

And what are these alien policemen doing swarming all over the place?'

Golightly quickly explained about the Judoon and their search for the Invisible Assassin. The Doctor could see that Salter was far from impressed.

'That's all we need – dead passengers and alien policemen. This is getting beyond a joke.'

'The Doctor here's going to try and help,' Golightly told him.

Salter gave the Doctor an intense look. 'And what are you – some kind of crisis management expert?'

The Doctor scratched the back of his neck. 'No, well, yes, maybe I am. Crisis management, yes I suppose that's what I do, although I'm not sure about the management bit, sounds a bit desk-bound – meetings and agendas and all that, and no offence to you, Mr Golightly, but that's not really me.'

Salter stared at the man in amazement. How could anyone talk that fast for so long and say nothing?

'So can you help with this crisis or not?' he demanded.

'Of course I can. But first I need my... er... equipment. It's a big blue box. Perhaps General Moret could take me back to where he found me?'

'I'll organise it right away,' promised Golightly. 'But you'll need to clear it with your Judoon pals.'

'They're no friends of mine, believe me,' the Doctor assured him. 'But I'm sure they can be persuaded to cooperate. They're pretty monocular types – only interested in their own agenda.'

He looked over at Salter, who was staring down at the

arrivals hall, with a furious expression on his face.

'There's a lot of it about,' concluded the Doctor under his breath.

The offices of the Jupiter Detective Agency were not particularly impressive, but Nikki had become used to them. Her father didn't think the physical appearance of the office was that important and that was that.

'If people are going to select a detective agency on the basis of how luxurious the sofa in reception is,' he had said the last time Nikki had suggested a makeover, 'then I don't want to do business with them.' So the first impression a client got was of a company that didn't waste money. The carpet was a little worn, the desk and chairs in reception utilitarian. The only decoration on the walls was their official licence to operate a detective agency. 'Clients want results, not pretty pictures,' Nikki's dad liked to say, and certainly the clients they got were always very satisfied with the quality of the service. The only problem was that there weren't that many clients.

Nikki was pondering the problems of the agency as she made her way back to the office. Perhaps it wasn't the decor of the office that was the problem, perhaps it was the building itself, not to mention the neighbourhood. As she approached the dreary plain block, she found herself passing boarded-up shops and a couple of vagrants sleeping in doorways. This was the Lower East Side of the city, an area that had been up-and-coming eighty years ago. These days, the people had upped and gone, at least those with the economic muscle to move on. Those without much in the way of capital had no option but to remain, left behind and forgotten. There was talk of regeneration in the newsfeeds, but whenever decisions had to be made the investment seemed to go to the spaceport rather than the city.

The building that housed the family business was a four-storey brownstone, full of small office units hired out to all sorts of small and usually struggling businesses. The turnover rate was very high as the music teachers, software writers, lone accountants and estate agents established businesses, hit hard times and then, inevitably, failed and went bankrupt. Nikki and her dad had been there for five years, and she was fairly sure they were the longest-standing tenants.

Nikki pushed open the street doors and made her way through the lobby. Once the building had maintained its own reception, but the desk hadn't been manned for years. A panel of metallic business names listed the companies that had once occupied the building but now most people just taped a letter heading and floor number on the wall next to the lift.

When she got back inside the agency office on the third floor, the first thing Nikki did was to check for any messages. To her disappointment there was nothing new from her father. Nikki resolved to ignore his standing instructions and open his case file if he didn't get in touch in the next twenty-four hours.

The phone rang and Nikki picked up the receiver with a thrill of excitement. Could this be him now?

'Jupiter Detective Agency,' she trilled in her best

receptionist voice. 'How may I help you?' She tried to hide her frustration when the voice at the other end of the line was female and clearly not her dad.

'May I speak to Detective Jupiter, please?' asked the woman. Nikki would have placed the owner of the voice in her seventies or eighties. There was a hint of an accent to the voice as well, but Nikki wasn't sure that she could identify it. Off-world perhaps.

Nikki politely explained that the Mr Jupiter wasn't available but perhaps 'one of his associates' could help. The old lady hesitated and confided in Nikki that she didn't want to be a problem. Perhaps she could try again in a day or two. Nikki knew that the agency could really do with the work – and the income – and suggested that she should come in as soon as possible.

'If you have a problem that requires a detective then you can't afford to waste time,' she told the old lady, hoping she wasn't overdoing it. 'Time is of the essence in any investigation. Trails can go cold.'

For a moment there was no sound from the other end of the line and Nikki feared that she had gone too far but then the old lady spoke again.

'Maybe you're right. Is it possible to make an appointment to see one of Mr Jupiter's associates?'

'Let me check,' Nikki said, relieved. She put the receiver down on the desktop and then flicked through a diary close to the mouthpiece. There were, of course, no associates; just Nikki's dad and herself, but she wasn't going to admit that to a potential client. After a beat she picked up the receiver.

'One of Mr Jupiter's junior associates could see you in an hour's time if you can get here,' she told the woman, who happily accepted the appointment.

Nikki put the phone down and smiled to herself. If Dad was going to keep going off like this, then she'd have to start opening her own case files, and the little old lady's mystery – whatever it proved to be – could be her first entirely solo case.

The security officer had escorted the Doctor back through the various corridors and passageways of the backstage baggage area without talking to him once. A couple of times they were challenged by Judoon, but General Moret had been able to use his credentials to gain them free passage to continue. He did not do it with much charm, however. The Doctor could see that the security man was not at all happy at the sight of aliens overrunning his territory.

'You're thinking that if they just told you more about what they were looking for you might be able to help, aren't you?' murmured the Doctor.

Moret just shrugged.

'Trouble is they don't work like that,' the Doctor continued, ignoring the cold shoulder. 'They have their methods and they like to keep to them.'

'Inefficient,' muttered Moret. 'Cack-handed, overbearing, unsubtle...'

'Not impressed, I take it?' replied the Doctor.

Moret grunted. 'That's what people used to say about me,' he confessed, to the Doctor's surprise. 'Ex-Space

Marine coming into civilian security. Everyone thought I'd try to run things like we do in the military. And they were right – at first. But I soon learned otherwise.'

'I'm afraid the Judoon aren't too hot on learning new tricks,' the Doctor told him.

'More's the shame,' Moret stopped and opened a door. 'Here we are.'

The Doctor stepped through the doorway and found himself in the loading area where the TARDIS had landed just hours earlier.

'It's not here!' he exclaimed.

'What?' Moret came through the door behind him and saw for himself. The area where the TARDIS had been standing was completely empty.

'Someone must have moved it,' the Doctor suggested.

Moret shook his head. 'Baggage systems were all offline. Nothing down here could have moved a box the size you described.'

The Doctor turned on him. 'So where is it then?'

The security officer shrugged. 'Guess it's just one more piece of lost luggage.'

'What?'

'Haven't you been paying attention, Doctor? It's been happening for days. As well as all the delays and other glitches, we've lost track of hundreds of pieces of luggage. Until that tourist exploded and those rhinos turned up, tracking down the missing luggage was priority number one,' he explained.

The Doctor was deep in thought. 'So the new terminal has glitches and delays, people's luggage goes missing and then you have a passenger explode in one of the toilets. Three different problems.'

'Four if you add whatever it is those rhinos are after,' Moret pointed out.

The Doctor, thick-rimmed glasses on, was examining the space where the TARDIS had been standing. 'Bit of a coincidence, though, isn't it? Four different mysteries, same location.'

'What are you suggesting?' asked the security officer.

The Doctor stood up and returned his glasses to his pocket. 'I don't know what I'm suggesting,' he confessed, 'at least not yet. I'm just following a train of thought. And it's making me suspicious. All these things; all happening in this one terminal…' A thought struck him. 'What about Terminals One to Twelve. How's business with them?'

'Well, Terminal Three closed years back and Terminal Eight's out of commission pending refurbishment, but the others are all working normally,' Moret informed the Doctor.

'No exploding passengers, no luggage going walkies?'

Moret shook his head. 'Nothing out of the ordinary at all, far as I know.'

'Then all this,' the Doctor waved an arm around airily, 'all this happening at Terminal 13. That's got to be more than just bad luck, hasn't it?'

'So what are you going to do about it?' wondered the security officer.

The Doctor grinned. 'Get to the bottom of it, of course. Find out what's really going on. Oh I love a good mystery me. Love four even more.'

He headed back through the doorway and then, without missing a beat, popped his head back through again. 'Although, if I'm completely honest, I could have done without the bloke exploding.' And then he was gone again, and the security officer found he had to run to catch up with the annoying stranger.

When they got back to the General Manager's Office, the Judoon Commander was already there.

'They haven't found what they were looking for,' Golightly told the Doctor and Moret as they came into the room.

'Correction,' the Judoon interrupted. 'We have not found it *yet*. We have not concluded our business here.'

'I thought you said you had completed your search?' spluttered Golightly indignantly.

'We have completed our search of Terminal 13. The other Terminals have fully functioning security logs which have also been scanned and checked. There is only one logical conclusion: our quarry has managed to escape directly from this terminal into the city outside this facility.'

'But you checked every passenger,' Moret pointed out. 'Are you saying someone evaded your search?'

The Judoon swung his massive head around to look at the human security officer.

'It is the only possible explanation. We must move our search into New Memphis itself!'

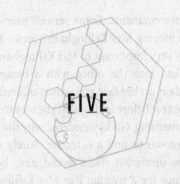

FIVE

Nikki's meeting with her client did not begin well. As soon as Mrs Kellingham arrived at the Jupiter Detective Agency office, Nikki could see that the old woman was having second thoughts.

Nikki was pleased to see that she had been right about the voice. Mrs Kellingham was certainly an old lady, though probably nearer to ninety than eighty. With the latest rejuvenation technology, humans routinely lived longer lives than ever before and to the untrained eye it was difficult to put an age on many older people, but Nikki's dad had pointed out to her the telltale signs to look for. Wrinkles could be ironed out, he used to tell her, but you can always see the tracks of the surgeon's knife.

Mrs Kellingham was a case in point. At first glance she looked like a woman in her fifties – auburn hair, smooth skin, sparkling eyes – but Nikki could see through the cosmetic improvements. Some serious money had been spent on achieving Mrs Kellingham's look. Appearances were clearly very important to Mrs Kellingham.

She walked into the office with a barely concealed look of disdain on her face and, when offered a chair, she brushed the seat before sitting as if she was worried about catching something. Nikki wondered why the woman had come downtown to find a detective. Surely one of their larger, more upmarket rivals would have been a more natural choice for a woman like Mrs Kellingham. Once this thought had occurred to Nikki, it nagged away at the corner of her mind as she began the usual introduction to the detective agency's working methods, fees and payment system. But Mrs Kellingham waved the standard contract away. She dropped an impressive-looking diamond onto the desk.

'Worth five thousand credits at least,' she told the young detective simply. 'Yours if you complete the case.'

Nikki took up the gem and looked at it. To her untrained eye it looked genuine enough, but she'd get it checked by her jewellery client nonetheless.

'It's a little unorthodox—' she began, but again the old lady interrupted her.

'I've no time for contracts and paperwork. I'm not getting any younger. I want results, and I'm prepared to pay for them.'

'Is that why you chose us, not one of the bigger agencies?' Nikki regretted the question as soon as she'd asked it. It was both rude and foolish, and she could see from Mrs Kellingham's reaction that she was taken aback.

'If you don't want the case…' she said, reaching forward for the gem.

Nikki closed her fingers over the diamond. 'Oh no, I didn't mean to suggest that,' she insisted. 'Of course I, we, want the job.'

Mrs Kellingham looked at her coolly for a moment, her eyes narrowing.

'I admire your honesty,' she said finally. 'I can see that you need the work.'

'We're moving to new uptown premises soon,' improvised Nikki, aware of the drabness of the office.

'I'm sure you are. Find what was stolen from me and I'll make sure it happens. Call it a bonus.'

Nikki's mouth hung open. *Was Mrs Kellingham really offering her new offices?*

'I own a lot of property uptown,' the older women explained. 'Now, do you want to hear about my problem or should I take my business elsewhere?'

Nikki picked up her notepad and pen and began making notes. Mrs Kellingham explained that she had recently been on an off-world trip, a long luxury cruise that had taken her away for twelve months. When she had returned, just a couple of days earlier, she had come through Terminal 13 at Elvis the King Spaceport.

Nikki made what she hoped were the appropriate sympathetic noises, and enquired as to what kind of delays Mrs Kellingham had been forced to endure.

The older lady shrugged. 'No worse than any other spaceport,' she told the girl. 'When you've travelled as much as I have, you get used to delays. Standing in line isn't a problem, but becoming a victim of street crime *is*.'

Nikki frowned. 'Street crime?' she asked.

Mrs Kellingham nodded. 'A pickpocket, I think.'

'And what did he take from you?'

To Nikki's surprise, for the first time since she had entered the room Mrs Kellingham hesitated and looked, well, a little embarrassed. Nikki was intrigued. *What had the old woman been carrying?*

'I must confess,' continued her client eventually, 'I do feel a bit of a fool.'

'I don't understand,' Nikki told her, her pen poised over the notepad ready to take down whatever Mrs Kellingham was about to say.

'It's a watch. An old-fashioned mechanical timepiece.'

Nikki still looked a little blank. 'An old watch,' she repeated, writing it down.

'Not just an old watch. A valuable family heirloom. Handmade on Earth eight hundred years ago.'

'So it's an antique?'

Mrs Kellingham nodded simply. 'A priceless antique. Swiss-made, and in perfect working order. It's beautiful.'

'And you carry this valuable antique when you travel?' Nikki couldn't keep the note of incredulity out of her question.

'I'm an old woman,' retorted Mrs Kellingham sharply. 'If I have something beautiful I want to see it, not have it locked away in a vault somewhere. It can do that when I'm dead and gone.'

Feeling admonished, Nikki apologised. 'I didn't mean to be rude,' she explained.

The old lady's expression softened. 'No need to apologise. It was a reasonable enough question. Put it down to an old fool's arrogance. I never for one moment considered anyone would try to take it from me.'

'But someone did?'

'I assume so. It disappeared. I know I had it on when I came through passport control, but when I reached my driver it was no longer on my wrist.'

Nikki thought for a moment. 'That does sound like the work of a pickpocket. Did anyone bump into you when you were walking through the airport?'

Now it was Mrs Kellingham's turn to think. 'Yes, yes there was one incident,' she said after a beat. 'Someone backed into me when I was looking for my driver.'

Nikki leant forward. 'Do you remember anything about this someone?' she wondered.

'Why, yes,' Mrs Kellingham smiled. 'He was so apologetic, he was almost beside himself with embarrassment. He helped me to a seat and made sure I was all right…' She trailed off. 'You don't think he… But I never felt a thing.' Once again Mrs Kellingham flushed with embarrassment. 'I said I was a fool,' she reminded Nikki in a much less commanding tone.

Nikki couldn't help but feel sorry for her. She was a proud woman, and yet she had fallen for one of the oldest tricks in the book.

'Is there anything you can remember about the man – about the way he looked?' she asked gently.

Mrs Kellingham looked up sharply. 'He had blue skin. Does that help?'

Nikki smiled warmly. Perhaps this would be easier than she'd first thought.

'The problem is, this isn't going to be easy.'

The Doctor had been arguing with the Judoon Commander for some time now and, as far as Jase Golightly could make out, he didn't seem to be making any headway.

'Further Judoon squads can be here within two days. With enough officers, we can extend our search,' insisted the Judoon.

'Haven't you been listening to a word I've been saying?' the Doctor asked rhetorically. 'Searching the spaceport was one thing, but that's a city out there. Homes and businesses and warehouses. Alleys and crannies and nooks and all sorts. Your usual methods aren't going to work out there.'

'Justice must be swift,' the Judoon stated, not for the first time.

'Well, it's not going to be very swift if you hang around waiting for reinforcements, is it?' suggested the Doctor. 'Look, the majority of the population here is human. I know humans. I've spent a lot of time with humans. I know how they think and how they deal with things. Let me go into the city and follow the trail before it goes cold. I'll find your quarry.'

The Judoon considered for a moment and then took a step closer to the Doctor.

'Why would you do this?' he asked.

The Doctor shrugged. 'Because I want answers. Because

I don't want Judoon terrorising the city. Because someone's stolen my TARDIS and I want it back.'

'Ah,' exclaimed the Judoon as the Doctor reached the end of his list. 'Self-interest. I understand that motivation. But this is also a matter of honour. The Judoon cannot stand by and have another party complete our mission.'

The Judoon turned and began to walk out of the office.

'Wait,' cried the Doctor.

The Judoon paused in the doorway.

'How about a compromise?' the Doctor suggested.

'What manner of compromise?'

The Doctor hurried across the room to look the Commander in the eye. 'You send your Judoon back to your ships to wait. Then you and I go into the city to find your man. Give us, what, let's say forty-eight hours. That gives us two days to gets results with some good old-fashioned detective work. If we get no leads in forty-eight hours, when your reinforcements arrive, then you do it your way.'

The Doctor watched as the Judoon Commander considered the proposal. It really was uncanny how like a rhino a Judoon really was. The wide lipless mouth, the rows of yellowing teeth, the two horns and flared nostrils, and, perched on top of the head, two little comedy ears. Not for the first time, he wondered what kind of world had evolved a life form like the Judoon. One day he'd have to find out. If he ever got the TARDIS back, he reminded himself, bringing himself back to the present.

'You and I go into the city alone?' the Judoon asked.

'Not scared are you?' joked the Doctor.

'Judoon are not frightened of anything,' the alien retorted. 'I will accept your suggestion.'

The Doctor smiled, but then the Judoon continued to speak.

'But with one amendment. I will allow twenty-four hours only for the two of us to complete the mission. I will arrange the withdrawal of all Judoon.'

The Commander stepped out of the office to pass the new orders on to the rest of the Judoon.

Golightly, who had been listening to the exchange from behind his desk, jumped to his feet and came over to congratulate the Doctor.

'As soon as those creatures go, I can get the repair teams in. You were right, Doctor. This is going to give us a chance to get back on top of things.'

The Doctor didn't look quite so happy. 'Assuming my new friend and I can make some progress in the next twenty-four hours.'

Golightly sighed. 'I was trying to forget about that bit,' he confessed. 'Where will you start?'

The Doctor pushed a hand through his unruly hair. 'With the exploding man, I suppose. We need to find out who he was.'

Nikki had hit the ground running. As soon as Mrs Kellingham left the office, Nikki got on the phone to her contact at police headquarters. The New Memphis Police weren't the most efficient police service in the sector and much of the organisation was riddled with corruption, but there were good men and women scattered through the ranks and Janne Hoffenham was one of them. She was also Nikki's godmother.

In the difficult years since Nikki's mother had died, Janne had been the most important woman in Nikki's life. She had once been her father's partner at work. When Nikki's dad had left the police to set up the detective agency, Janne had remained in the force and she'd been a useful contact over the years.

Janne had checked with the police computer and, as Nikki had hoped, confirmed that there weren't that many blue-skinned pickpockets on the books. In fact there was just one – Horat Deselup. Although concentrating on her own case, Nikki couldn't miss the opportunity to see if Janne had heard from her father at all, but her tentative question was met with an apologetic 'no'.

Putting her growing anxiety about her father's safety to the back of her mind, Nikki set off for the neighbourhood where Deselup was known to live. The police computer didn't have an exact address for the man, but it did have details of a bar he was known to frequent. Stopping only to pick up one of the fake IDs she hoped her father didn't know about, Nikki headed out.

At only seventeen, Nikki was hardly an expert on bars but she didn't need to have seen many to know that this particular joint – the Black Hole – was not especially upmarket. It was dark and gloomy and full of people who didn't seem overly bothered about either quality. The decoration was primitive: simple wooden furniture, bare wooden floor. Nikki was surprised that there wasn't a carpet of sawdust on the ground. A long wooden-topped bar ran along the length of one wall, with dozens of optics behind it. In the middle of the bar sat a gaudy, painted glass clown full of coins – some kind of charity box collection. Nikki noted with amusement that the punters here seemed to treat the collection box as some kind of good luck charm, dropping coins into it and then patting the clown's head.

Nikki ordered a cola and sat at a table near the door, nursing her drink. She didn't have to wait long. She watched carefully as customers ordered drinks and chatted to each other and noted that, periodically, the bar staff would carry trays of drinks into a back room though a wide swing door. When the door to this rear room was open, Nikki had a fleeting glimpse of some card tables picked out by low-hanging overhead spot lamps. According to the police records her godmother had accessed for her, gambling was Deselup's favourite occupation. If he wasn't already inside at one of the card tables, he was sure to arrive soon. Nikki was just beginning to think about ways to get herself inside the back room when the back door swung open and a couple of players emerged. One of them had blue skin. He was a tall thin man, with the long delicate fingers of a concert pianist. He moved with grace, seeming to almost float across the floor.

The blue-skinned man stopped at the bar to say goodnight to the barman and dropped a couple of coins into the charity box. Nikki took the opportunity to slip outside ahead of him. It would be easier to tail him undetected if she started ahead of him.

Once outside, she wandered over to a bus stop and

pretended to study the timetable. The printed sheet was protected by a plastic case, just reflective enough for Nikki to see the entrance to the bar behind her. A few moments later, the doors pushed open and the blue-skinned man emerged. He took off to the left, and Nikki began to move too. Keeping to her own side of the road she let him stay five or six paces ahead of her.

For five blocks they continued without incident. Nikki noted that they were moving back towards the spaceport. Suddenly she realised that the blue-skinned man had disappeared from sight. *How was that possible?* He'd been there a minute ago. Nikki quickly crossed the road to the side where her man had been walking but there was no sign of him. *Had he doubled back? Was it possible that he had spotted her?*

Nikki turned around and went back over the route the man had just passed. Suddenly someone grabbed her by the arm and pulled her into a doorway.

'Lost something?' hissed a voice.

Nikki twisted her head to see the man holding her. Even in the dim light, the blue skin was unmistakable. It was Deselup.

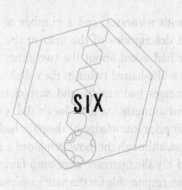

SIX

'Keep your eyes open,' suggested the Doctor as he and the Judoon Commander walked towards the taxi rank outside the spaceport entrance.

'For what?' grunted the Judoon, who was still not convinced that he was doing the right thing.

'Anything,' replied the Doctor.

Inside the massive terminals of the spaceport the atmosphere was regulated, but out in the open the Doctor was grateful for his heavy coat. It was cold, windy and wet. The lights of the city twinkled in the rain, giving it a fairy-tale ambience, but the Doctor wasn't fooled for a moment.

There hadn't been much in the way of evidence from the remains of the exploding man. His clothes were no more than a few scraps of burnt material and there were no surviving documents of any kind. They had been more fortunate with witnesses, and a number of people had given good descriptions of the man in the café. When the Doctor had asked about the two other men at the table – the white-haired twins in their dark suits – most of the witnesses had rapidly and suspiciously suffered a convenient amnesia. At least locals did. Off-worlders, who had no prior knowledge of the pair, had been more talkative and, although the 'how' remained a mystery, the Doctor and his alien partner were both fairly sure about *who* had been responsible for the man's violent death.

'But this murder is a local matter for local law enforcement,' the Judoon complained when the Doctor explained his thinking. The Doctor shook his head firmly.

'It's all part of the bigger picture,' the Doctor insisted. 'Don't leap to conclusions and don't ignore anything. That's the secret of a great detective.'

'Detective work is slow; justice should be swift,' retorted the Judoon.

'Don't start that again,' the Doctor urged him.

Armed with an image of the dead man from the security cameras, he and the Judoon Commander had talked to the passport and customs officer on duty in Terminal 13 to see if anyone recognised him. The imposing figure of the Judoon thrusting the printout of the man under the nose of each customs officer was not a great success. Having the massive horned head of an alien looming over them had the unfortunate side effect of causing sudden and complete memory loss. Twenty-year customs veterans were left quivering wrecks after being exposed to the demanding interrogation techniques of the Judoon. Eventually, the Doctor intervened and his calmer, less accusatory approach had eventually produced a result.

They had a name: Aroon Manish. They knew what flight he had come in on. What they didn't know was where his luggage was.

'Perhaps these brothers took it,' suggested the Judoon Commander. 'We must locate them.'

The Doctor agreed and, after taking advice from General Moret about how to go about things, they set off for Police Headquarters.

'Watch your backs there, Doctor,' the security man advised as he escorted them to the main entrance of the spaceport.

'You're not suggesting we shouldn't trust the police, are you?' grinned the Doctor. The General's lack of reply spoke volumes.

The Judoon Commander was less amused. 'Law enforcers must be honourable and honest,' he insisted.

'Of course they should,' agreed the Doctor, 'but in places like New Memphis there are no guarantees.'

Not for the first time in her young life, Nikki was grateful for the martial arts lessons that her father had signed her up for at an early age. Keen that his daughter should grow up able to defend herself, he had insisted that she start lessons as soon as she could walk. And Nikki had taken to the discipline like a duck to water. She had only allowed herself to be grabbed and dragged into the dark doorway because the coward had attacked without warning, but now it was time to go on the offensive.

'Why are you following me?' hissed the voice. She could hear the tension in his voice. He was scared. *Why would a man like this be scared of a seventeen-year-old girl?* Nikki tensed her muscles ready to make a move, but held back for a moment, realising that this was an opportunity.

'Who said I was following you?' she replied calmly, interested to see his response.

He tightened his grip on her arms, which he held behind her back. 'Don't treat me like an idiot, I know when I'm being followed. Are you with the Widow?'

'You think I'd tell you if I was,' she replied haughtily.

Her ploy worked, and the man released her, pushing her forward. She spun round to get a good look at her assailant. If his voice had sounded scared a moment ago, it was nothing to the expression on his face now.

'You tell Yilonda I'm strictly freelance. I'm not taking sides in no gang war,' the blue-skinned man insisted, his eyes wide with fear. 'You got that? Make sure you tell her!' With that, he turned and ran off. He dashed right into the road and managed to duck and dance his way between the hooting traffic and then disappeared up an alley on the far side.

Nikki grinned. That had been more successful than she could have expected. She didn't know what it all meant yet but she was sure it would be useful intelligence in time. In the meantime, she had something else to aid her search. While the pickpocket had held her tight she had turned the tables on him. Using skills that matched his own, she had slipped a tiny tracking device into his jacket pocket. She activated her wrist-puter and searched for the signal.

A blip announced the successful acquisition of the signal, and a tiny blue dot appeared on the screen. The blue-skinned man could run as much as he liked; Nikki now knew his every move.

The gleaming tower that housed the Police HQ had promised much, but the reality had been a crushing disappointment. The Doctor and the Judoon Commander had been passed from office to office, from waiting room to waiting room, without actually seeing anything in the way of a serving police officer. The civilian administrators were polite but useless to the investigators. The Doctor was beginning to lose his patience but, unsurprisingly, it was the Judoon Commander who lost his temper first.

He jumped up from the seat where they'd been asked, once again, to wait and thrust his massive head through the small window behind which the latest receptionist was sitting. Seeing the rhino-headed alien coming towards her, the unfortunate girl had screamed and tried to jump out of her own chair but she got tangled up in the wire from her headset and fell back into her seat.

'We must see an officer NOW!' barked the Judoon. 'We will not tolerate any further delays.'

'And we will not tolerate alien police operating outside their jurisdiction,' added a new voice.

The Judoon and the Doctor both turned to see a non-uniformed police officer coming to meet them. The woman was fifty-something, dark haired and carrying a little more weight than was recommended for a humanoid of her height.

'Detective Angie Corilli,' she told them, thrusting out a hand to shake. 'And I'd appreciate it if you didn't intimidate the secretarial staff. You know how difficult it is to recruit a kid who can actually file stuff? Come this way.'

The Doctor was amused to see that even his alien colleague was rendered speechless by this. The Judoon Commander looked at him, and he shrugged before walking in the direction the woman had indicated. They followed her down a narrow corridor from which numerous small offices could be accessed. The Judoon's wide shoulders brushed the walls, dislodging posters and pictures as he passed.

Finally Corilli led them into her office. 'Pardon the mess,' she muttered as she moved a pile of files off one of the two guest chairs on one side of the desk, which itself was all but covered with paperwork. She glanced up at the Judoon who was wedged in the doorway. 'I don't think these chairs are large enough for you,' she said, a little embarrassed.

'I shall stand here, then,' replied the Judoon with as much dignity as he could muster. The Doctor, however, happily plopped himself into the chair, swinging his legs up to hang over the arm on one side.

'Right then, tell us everything you know,' he suggested.

Corilli laughed. 'How long have you got?' she joked.

The whole room shook as the Judoon in the doorway stomped his feet. 'Justice is swift. Not funny,' he announced.

'You'll have to excuse my friend,' the Doctor told the detective. 'He's a bit keen.'

'I've worked with the type before,' confessed Corilli.

The room shook again. Corilli looked over at the Judoon with a pained expression. 'Please don't do that. These are merely partition walls. It won't take much to bring the whole lot down.'

'Then do not waste my time,' warned the Judoon. 'Tell us about the human twins in the dark suits.'

'The Walinski brothers – Uncle's top goons.'

'Uncle?' repeated the Doctor. 'Who's "Uncle"?'

'Bad news squared,' replied the detective, reaching for a phone. 'Let me get someone in here who can tell you all about him…'

The Casino was housed in a striking modern building at the edge of the hotel district that ran in a thin strip like a buffer between the spaceport and the rest of downtown New Memphis. This was the tourist-trap part of town, an area where bars, clubs and shops never closed. It was a place of constant noise: people, music, traffic – a district where darkness never fell.

Nikki loathed it. She was much happier in the dark and grotty downtown backstreets, with their dangerous shadows and endless rain. Here in the bright lights, Nikki found the atmosphere electric, and not in a good way. It felt like she was on a movie set; everyone was just a little bit too happy, too garrulous, too excited. As far as Nikki was concerned, it was as unnatural as the multicoloured neon lights that adorned every building.

The Casino – or, to give it its full title, the New Memphis Grand Casino and Gaming Hall – was lit up so much that it was difficult to look at it for too long without risking permanent damage to your eyes. It was a magnet for anyone with adventure in their hearts and money in their wallets, and the management happily opened its doors to any, human and alien alike, who wished to spend a little time and a lot of cash at any of the gaming tables within. The only exception was the age rule. It was strictly over twenty-ones only.

Nikki looked at her reflection in a shop window. She was wearing her usual work clothes: a light jacket, old jeans, sneakers. Her blonde hair was pulled back in a simple bunch and a tea-cosy-like green hat sat on her head. She wasn't wearing any make-up to speak of and, although she was carrying plenty of ID that would qualify her to get inside, there was no way her current appearance would match any of the fake identities. She glanced at the wrist-puter again, and the blue flashing blip of light confirmed that her quarry had entered the Casino. No ID problem for him! Nikki sighed and turned away. She needed to find another way in and quickly.

Corilli had summoned another cop to fill the Doctor and the Judoon Commander in on the Walinski brothers and their employer, the mysterious 'Uncle'. Detective Dantin was small and wiry, with a scruffy unshaven appearance. Passing him in the street, you might mistake him for a homeless vagrant rather than a police officer, but Corilli assured her guests that Dantin was one of the best.

'Ten years working organised crime in this city,' Corilli told them. 'What he doesn't know about Uncle isn't worth knowing.'

'Except how to put the creep behind bars,' grumbled Dantin miserably. The Doctor wondered how many years it had been since the man had last smiled; his face had an expression of barely contained anger that looked pretty permanent. He leant against the wall and folded his arms, chewing on a toothpick.

'So this Uncle… local Mr Big, is he?' prompted the Doctor, hoping to get the man talking again.

'You could say that,' replied Dantin, pulling the toothpick from his mouth and flicking it, without success, in the direction of Corilli's overflowing bin. 'Most cities have a guy like him. Likes to think of himself as a businessman, calls himself an entrepreneur. Which is fancy language for crook, if you ask me. He has some legit operations, of course, the Casino, a property portfolio, that kind of thing, but that's just a smokescreen for the real stuff. Protection, drugs, smuggling, people-trafficking… He has his fingers in pretty much every criminal pie going. That's why he's the Uncle.'

'And the brothers?' The question rumbled out of the Judoon's mouth suddenly. The Doctor realised that subconsciously both Corilli and Dantin had been addressing themselves almost exclusively to him, as if by not looking at the massive alien in the room they could pretend he didn't exist. The Doctor smiled to himself; he'd heard of the elephant in the room, but rarely the rhino.

Dantin cleared his throat and made a visible effort to look the Judoon in the eye as he spoke. Corilli looked away, preferring to read some of the backed-up paperwork on her desk.

'The Walinski brothers. Albino twins. Human, not that you'd notice. Cold, ruthless, violent, deadly.'

'Sounds like all too many humans, if you ask me,' commented the Doctor.

Dantin ignored the interruption. 'They're Uncle's right-hand men, his enforcers, his most loyal men.'

The Doctor frowned. 'So what are Uncle's top dogs doing at the spaceport on a routine meet and greet?' he wondered. The question hung in the air for a second, and then the Doctor provided his own answer. 'Whatever else it was, it wasn't a routine meeting. Can't have been.'

'We will ask this Uncle why the brothers were at the spaceport,' suggested the Judoon Commander.

Dantin snorted. 'Yeah, like that's going to happen.'

The Doctor shot him a sharp look. 'Why not take the direct approach?' he wondered. 'Where do we find Uncle then?'

The Doctor was amused to see the surprise on Dantin's face. It looked as if he couldn't believe what he'd just heard.

'What are you going to do? Walk up to Uncle and ask him to help you with your enquiries?'

'Why not?' grinned the Doctor.

Dantin shook his head sadly, clearly giving up on them. 'The Grand Casino,' he said simply. 'Grab a taxi. Even the off-planet ming-mongs that drive most of the taxis round here know how to find the Casino.'

Corilli looked up as Dantin gave the visitors a mock salute, then shuffled out of the office.

The Doctor got to his feet.

'If you don't mind, I am kinda busy,' she said.

The Doctor nodded and thanked her for her time.

Keeping her eyes on their backs as he and the Judoon disappeared down the corridor, Corilli reached for the phone and dialled a stored number.

'We may have a problem,' she whispered into the phone receiver urgently.

SEVEN

Nikki put on her best smile and tried to stand tall with confidence – but it was far from easy. The uniform for the female staff at the Casino had many features that were not to Nikki's taste, but the high-heeled shoes were definitely her least favourite. Then there was the skirt that was so short it could have doubled as a belt.

Nikki looked at herself in the mirror and took a deep breath. With the costume – such as it was – and a serious amount of make-up, she reckoned she could pass herself off as one of the glamorous cocktail waitresses who serviced the high-rollers. As long as she didn't totter in the heels too much and give herself away. Nikki pushed open the door and set about playing her newly acquired role. She hoped the poor girl she'd borrowed the uniform and security pass from wouldn't get into too much trouble. She'd been keen enough to take Nikki's money and, while far from bright, she had clearly understood that this opportunity to get a night off at double pay was something she'd need to keep secret.

Out in the gaming halls, Nikki quickly realised she'd made the right decision. Despite the almost indecent clothing the girls wore, they seemed to be all but invisible. The clients would snap their fingers and order drinks and snacks, but they rarely gave the serving girls a second glance, keeping their focus firmly on the gaming tables in front of them. Nikki was quickly able to get the lay of the land, identifying the discreetly positioned security gorillas and the surveillance cameras.

There were five main gaming halls over two floors and twice as many bars. An extensive behind-the-scenes area made sure that everything ran smoothly and gave access to kitchens, storerooms and a security suite. Access to the first floor from the bottom was either by a breathtaking wall-free elevator or by a spectacular escalator that threaded through a clever artificial waterfall without getting the visitor wet. Nikki also located some lifts leading to the private upper floors from where Uncle ran his entire operation. It had been impossible to keep her wrist-puter on whilst wearing the staff uniform, but before she had changed she had confirmed that her blue-skinned friend was somewhere on the third floor. Somehow she had to get up there too.

The Doctor had decided to take a more direct approach than Nikki's.

'I think you should wait here,' he said to the Judoon

Commander when they reached the impressive-looking frontage of the Casino building. The Judoon looked for a moment as if he might argue the point, but then he nodded in agreement.

Leaving his alien partner to wait for him on the other side of the street, the Doctor simply presented himself at the main entrance.

'I'd like to speak to Uncle,' he said simply to the doorman.

'Go on, George, do as the man asks,' said a familiar voice. A moment later, Derek Salter appeared, wheeling himself out through a pair of automatic doors that led to the casino proper.

'How goes the investigation?' Salter asked the Doctor, bringing his wheelchair to a halt.

'Early days,' replied the Doctor in a non-committal manner.

'Well, if you need to speak to Uncle, George here will sort you out, won't you, George?'

The doorman – George – nodded nervously and turned to use an intercom.

'I didn't realise you and Uncle were old friends,' commented the Doctor conversationally.

'Oh, I wouldn't say we were that,' replied Salter, 'but I occasionally take a few credits off the old man at his tables. I'd call us acquaintances rather than friends. Be seeing you.'

And with that cheery farewell, Salter wheeled off into the night. George the doorman came across to the Doctor and led him inside. As he passed through the automatic doors, the Doctor cast one last glance over his shoulder at the distant figure of the Judoon Commander, lurking in the shadows on the far side of the street. He hoped the alien law enforcer's patience would hold out.

The Doctor was escorted through the gaming halls towards the private lifts which would take him directly into Uncle's personal apartment. As he moved through the gaming halls, the Doctor scanned the rooms, carefully taking in the scene. One of the waitresses caught his eye as she stumbled in her heels, and the Doctor put out a hand to steady her. The girl blushed and thanked him in a quiet voice and then turned quickly away without making eye contact. The Doctor was puzzled by her body language; the girl seemed unduly tense.

'Problem, sir?' asked the doorman, aware that the Doctor had stopped walking. He followed the stranger's gaze and saw that he was looking at one of the waiting staff. 'Interesting uniforms, eh?' he commented.

'Look a bit chilly to me,' commented the Doctor, turning back to his escort. '*Allons-y*, George, don't want to keep Uncle waiting, do we?'

Nikki hurried to a table and leant on it heavily. That had been close. *Why had the stranger looked at her like that? Did he know something?* Pulling herself together, she looked back over shoulder at the new arrival being escorted through the halls. He was humanoid, and dressed in a slightly scruffy pinstriped suit, an outfit that might have looked more respectable but for the sneakers on his feet. He was following the doorman with his hands in his pockets, walking casually but, she noted, looking around him the whole time. Nikki's late mother had been a sensitive, but Nikki had never had any psychic twinges herself, at least not until today. There was something about the stranger, something deep and mysterious, that was fascinating; he seemed to have an invisible aura that drew her attention. She found herself moving across the room on a parallel course, keeping pace with him as he followed the doorman around the gaming tables.

She realised that he was being taken towards the private lifts, exactly where she wanted to go herself. She started clearing a table but continued to keep an eye on the stranger. She watched carefully as the doorman used a numerical keypad to call the lift. Automatically, Nikki memorised the code and watched as the man stepped into the lift. The doors began to close and her heart skipped a beat as he gave a little wave just before the doors closed. The doorman thought the wave was meant for him and gave a half-hearted salute in return, but Nikki knew that the stranger had been looking directly at her. *How had he known she was looking? Did he suspect she didn't belong there? And, more importantly, was he going to give her away?*

When the doors opened, the Doctor was not surprised to be met by Uncle in person. Introducing yourself to a crime lord by demanding a face-to-face visit without warning was always going to appeal to his curiosity. What did surprise the Doctor was Uncle himself. The Doctor had met a lot of powerful men, women and aliens in his nine hundred-plus years of travelling, but Uncle wasn't the stereotypical megalomaniac that he might have been. In fact, he was charm personified: a smallish man in his sixties, with snow-white hair and a neatly trimmed grey beard.

The apartment itself, although expensively decorated and furnished, was tasteful and subtle rather than the over-the-top nightmare it might have been. The colours were muted, and sympathetic spot lighting made even the large rooms feel intimate. Works of art from all over the universe were displayed on the walls and in glass cases.

Uncle had greeted the Doctor like an old friend, shaking his hand and inviting him to take tea. He led the Doctor through to a sitting room where a servant was quietly setting down a tray containing a teapot, china, and a selection of cakes. A woman with long blonde hair, dressed in a pretty white cocktail dress, was sitting in one of the armchairs.

'My daughter, Hope,' Uncle introduced her with a wave of his arm. The young woman, who the Doctor judged to be in her thirties, got up to greet him. Her hand, when he took it to shake, felt tiny. She seemed out of place in the world of Uncle the crime lord, and the Doctor wondered what, if anything, she knew of her father's criminal activities.

The three of them sat and took tea, making polite conversation about the weather and the state of affairs at the spaceport. He seemed to know that the Doctor had only recently arrived on New Memphis and expressed the hope that he hadn't travelled through the new and troubled Terminal 13. The Doctor assured him he'd not been that unlucky. He drained his cup and, placing it carefully back on the saucer, decided to get the conversation on track.

As he explained that he was working as a consultant to both the spaceport authorities and the police, Hope sat up and took a real interest in the topic at hand, for the first time in their conversation.

'Really?' she exclaimed. 'How exciting. Much more exciting than my class of seven-year-olds.'

Uncle shot an annoyed look in the direction of his daughter. 'Hope is a teacher,' he explained to his visitor. 'But apart from her job she doesn't get out much. She's always been frail, and the pollution in the city plays havoc with her asthma.'

The Doctor noted a slight narrowing of Hope's eyes and wondered for a moment if she was going to say something. When nothing was forthcoming, he continued.

'I'm interested in tracking down a couple of your employees – the Walinski brothers?' he told Uncle. Uncle held the Doctor's gaze for a moment.

'Tall chaps, white hair, smart suits, twins…' continued the Doctor.

Uncle turned to his daughter. 'I suspect we're going to be talking boring business matters, my dear, why don't you leave us to it? No need for you to feign interest in what will doubtless be tedious in the extreme for you.'

The Doctor expected the girl to protest, but to his surprise she merely nodded demurely and got to her feet.

'If you gentlemen will excuse me then, I'll take my leave of you,' she said, smiling sweetly. Uncle watched as she left the room.

'Lovely girl,' he commented after she had gone, 'the spit of her mum but not half the brains.' Uncle turned back to look at the Doctor. 'And both totally innocent and ignorant about my business. Which is the way I want it to remain.' There was an undeniable undertone to his words.

For the first time, the Doctor was getting a glimpse of the real Uncle – the vicious crime lord lurking under the charming exterior.

Nikki stepped into the corridor from the private lift and breathed a sigh of relief as she realised that it was empty. She moved down the corridor and, hearing voices from behind one door, she hurried past it. Further along the corridor she came across what looked like a waiting area. There were a number of sofas and armchairs and low tables with magazines.

Sitting in one of the chairs, with his back towards Nikki, was the blue-skinned man. As she watched he got to his feet and began pacing. Nikki drew back against the wall, watching him carefully. He pulled out a communicator and dialled a number.

'It's me. I'm being jerked around here. I was about to put a deal to Uncle when he suddenly decided he had another more urgent meeting. I've been waiting here ages.'

Whoever was at the end of the line must have been speaking because Deselup shut up for a bit. He continued pacing, and Nikki had to quickly duck down behind one of the large sofas to avoid being seen. While there, she pulled off the painful high-heeled shoes and rubbed her sore ankles.

'I'm going to give him a bit longer, but if he doesn't show me a bit of respect,' continued the blue-skinned man, 'I'll just go to Yilonda and see if she'll pay. She already put someone on my tail.' With that, the man ended his call and sat back down in the nearest seat.

Unfortunately, it was the sofa Nikki was hiding behind. She felt it push back under his weight, shifting it further back towards the wall, squashing and trapping her.

Without his daughter in the room, Uncle had become a completely different man. The Doctor began to understand now why so many people were afraid of him.

'What do you want to know about the Walinski brothers, then?' Uncle demanded without further niceties.

The Doctor explained about the sightings of them at the spaceport and the mysterious death of the exploding man.

'Was there anything to link my men to this death?' asked Uncle bluntly.

'They were seen with the victim,' the Doctor explained. 'They shared a table with him in a spaceport café.'

'Hardly suspicious, though, is it?' Uncle was on his feet. 'Don't waste my time, Doctor. I don't know what you thought you were doing coming here on a fishing trip, but you have to get up a lot earlier to catch me out. My men were at the spaceport to meet an old friend who never showed up. They may well have spent some time in a café drinking coffee. They wasted the whole morning. People in my business don't like wasting time.'

The Doctor stood up and looked Uncle directly in the eyes. 'Which business is that then? The legit one or all your criminal activities?' he asked levelly.

Uncle just laughed. 'Get out of here before I let my lawyers loose on you for defamation.'

The blue-skinned man had finally run out of patience. Nikki watched him stalk away back to the lifts and was then able to emerge from her hiding place. Before she could set off in pursuit of Deselup, though, another door opened. Nikki turned and ran barefoot in the opposite direction, hoping no one would see her.

The corridor curved around, quickly taking her out of sight but to be sure she began trying the doors. Finding one unlocked, she yanked it open and tumbled inside.

It was someone's bedroom – a woman's if the decor was anything to go on. The room was all pink and white with soft furnishings. The carpet was thick pile and the bed was covered with a soft velvety bedspread. At the window, enormous braided curtains hung from just under the ceiling to floor level. These were tied back at each side of the window forming an ornate frame for the view out over the city.

Curiosity getting the better of her, Nikki began to look around. There was a massive dressing table covered with make-up and jewellery boxes and a huge mirror surrounded by individual light bulbs like a theatrical dressing room. There was one thing, however, that looked totally out of place. It was a small piece of technical kit about the size of a shoe. It had some buttons, dials, a small screen and a retractable aerial. Was it some sort of control device?

Suddenly in the mirror she saw the door beginning to open. She had seconds to look around for a hiding place.

Luckily, there was room behind the curtain.

Nikki held her breath as she heard the door creak open. There was no way to see anything in the room – all she could do was listen and hope that whoever it was just passed through. She strained to hear what was happening, cursing the thick carpet which muffled all footsteps. She heard the door close with a click but had the visitor come in or not?

Without warning, she got her answer as someone or something grabbed the curtain just above her head. Before she could react, the whole curtain, rail and all, was ripped from the wall and thrown aside by a creature unlike anything she had ever seen before. It was a giant humanoid alien with the massive twin-horned head of a rhinoceros.

Later, Nikki would be furious at the way she had reacted, but in the heat of the moment there was only one thing she could do. She screamed.

DOCTOR WHO

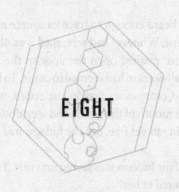

EIGHT

When the Doctor reached the lift doors, they opened for him. He stepped in, but as soon as the doors began to close he jumped out again and hurried off along the corridor. With a bit of luck, it would be a moment or two before Uncle's security staff noticed his disappearance. Just enough time for a quick poke around behind the scenes. When he had emerged from his meeting with Uncle, he had caught a glimpse of a figure running off down the corridor. He couldn't be certain, but he was fairly sure it was a woman wearing the house waitress uniform – almost certainly the young girl he'd seen in the gaming hall having balance problems with her shoes.

Taking the same route he'd seen the running girl take, the Doctor found himself walking down a curved corridor. A muffled scream suddenly sounded from somewhere close by. The sound was choked off in its prime, but the

Doctor had heard enough to trace its source to one of the nearest rooms. Whoever had screamed was silent now.

The Doctor pushed open the door to the room from which the half-scream had seemed to come. To his surprise, the Judoon Commander was in the room, with a hand covering the mouth of the girl he had seen downstairs. She was struggling to get free, but the Judoon had a good grip on her.

'Be quiet,' the Judoon was saying urgently. 'I do not wish to be discovered either!'

'Might be a bit late for that,' commented the Doctor, announcing his presence.

The girl and the Judoon both turned their heads to look at him.

'Doctor! What are you doing here?' exclaimed the Judoon.

'I could ask you the same thing,' replied the Doctor. 'You can let her go now,' he added. 'She's not going to scream again, are you?' He looked at the girl and gave her an encouraging smile.

The Judoon hesitated for a moment, just long enough to give the impression that what he was about to do was of his own volition rather than following the Doctor's orders, and then released the girl.

'Who are you people?' she demanded.

'I'm the Doctor,' the Doctor began brightly, 'and this is, er…' The Doctor stopped, for once in his life lost for words.

'I am Judoon Commander Rok Ma,' grunted the Judoon, rescuing the floundering Doctor. 'Galactic Law Enforcer.'

'You're cops!'

The Doctor shrugged, awkwardly. 'More sort of investigators,' he explained.

Nikki was relieved; at least they were on the right side, even if they were a little strange. She introduced herself and told them that she too was an investigator.

'I found something in here, something suspicious,' she told them, showing them the control device she'd found earlier. 'It doesn't look like it belongs here.'

The man who called himself the Doctor had slipped a pair of dark-rimmed spectacles onto his face and was examining the device with interest.

'What is it for?' wondered the Judoon.

'There's a time delay on it,' the Doctor told them, 'and whatever it is, it's about to go off.'

'Can't you switch it off?' Nikki asked.

'No time,' replied the Doctor, throwing the device onto the bed. 'Get down!'

The three of them took what cover they could as the Doctor called out the countdown.

'Five… four… three… two… one!'

Nikki wrapped her arms around her head, tucked herself into a ball and tensed, ready for something terrible to happen. For a long moment there was nothing but silence.

'That was a bit disappointing,' commented the Doctor sadly.

Suddenly an alarm began to ring, an instant clanging bell that was impossible to ignore.

'Either we've been discovered or that's the fire alarm,'

the Doctor mused. 'Us. Fire. I think we should… get out of here. C'mon, run!'

In the corridor, the reason for the alarm quickly became evident. Flames were bursting out of the room in which the Doctor had met Uncle, and thick billowing smoke was filling the corridor. There was no way to get to the lifts.

'We need to find another way out of here,' shouted the Doctor.

The Judoon pushed open a door. 'Stairs,' he announced.

'How did you know they were there?' asked Nikki incredulously as they started to run down the stairs.

'My ship scanned the building before I teleported in,' explained the Judoon Commander.

'You've got a teleport?' Nikki was fascinated. 'Can't you beam us all out of here then?'

The alien Judoon didn't break stride or turn to look at her. 'No,' he said simply.

'Oh, you haven't, have you?' groaned the Doctor. The Judoon looked at him impassively. 'You have,' the Doctor went on. 'You've sent your ship back into orbit. It's out of range.' He brightened. 'Oh well, always look on the bright side – no more Judoon teleporting in. Let's just hope we can get out.'

The trio reached the ground floor as he spoke, emerging into a scene of total chaos. The alarm was louder here, and it became immediately clear that the fire in the private apartments was not the only one. Thick black smoke filled the air, and a large area at the side of one of the gaming rooms was a mass of roaring flames. Screaming, panicking people were running for the exits, pushing each other out of the way in an effort to get out. A number of the staff were as frightened as the punters, but a few were trying to use emergency fire extinguishers to fight the fire.

The Doctor hurried to help, grabbing an extinguisher and beginning to aim the foam at the flames. He turned and saw that Nikki had turned her attention to the frightened people, helping them find their way through the chaos to the emergency exits. The Judoon Commander, however, was just standing like a statue, watching the chaos all around him. Was it possible the giant alien was afraid?

'Do something useful,' the Doctor shouted at the alien.

'This conflagration is containable,' the Judoon roared back at the Doctor. 'I have alerted local emergency services.'

'Bully for you,' the Doctor replied. 'But while we're waiting for Fireman Sam, people could lose their lives. We need to help.' The Doctor looked around, trying to make out what was happening. The smoke was getting quite dense now.

'There are people trapped over there,' the Doctor observed, waving an arm towards an area cut off from the rest of the room by a wall of flame. The Judoon looked in the direction the Doctor was indicating and then, without a moment's hesitation, he picked up a heavy gaming table and threw it down across the flames. For a moment the table acted like a blanket and muffled the flames. The quartet of gamblers who had been trapped hurried across the makeshift bridge to safety. The Judoon hauled the last of them clear as the table began to smoke and, seconds later, the flames returned, ripping through the wooden table top and reducing it to cinders.

The room was clearing now. Most of the public had escaped, leaving a handful of Casino staff fighting the fire alongside the Doctor and the Judoon Commander. Sirens roared from outside and soon they were joined by a professional fire-fighting crew. A powerful vacuum device began removing the smoke and numerous hoses began soaking the flames. The Doctor and the Judoon stepped to one side, with some relief, and let the trained fire-fighters take over. They carefully made their way through the abandoned chairs and tables of the gaming hall to the foyer. Here groups of people clustered nervously, recounting their individual stories of escape and checking their numbers. A few of them were still clutching gambling chips and beginning to ask about getting them cashed.

Nikki was perched on the main reception desk waiting for them.

'What caused it?' she wondered out loud as they walked over to join her.

'Incendiary device,' came the answer, but neither the Doctor nor the Judoon had provided it.

From out of the still-smoking Casino, the figure of Uncle appeared. His face was black, but from anger rather than the smoke. 'Someone set off a firebomb in my Casino!'

'Who would do a thing like that?' mused the Doctor.

'That damn Widow woman,' spat Uncle, furiously. 'But she's gone too far this time.'

The Doctor looked around. The fire-fighters seemed to have got the fire under control.

'Is everyone safe?' he asked.

A pained expression replaced the look of fury on Uncle's features.

'Hope!' he exclaimed. 'She was in the apartment but... I've not seen her.'

The Doctor was already running in the direction of the stairwell.

'Wait outside,' he shouted over his shoulder. 'I'll be back in a jiffy!'

The Doctor took the stairs two at a time. The fire seemed to have been contained on the ground floor but it was possible that no one knew about the fire in the private apartments.

He burst back into the corridor where the smoke was dissipating. When he approached the site of the fire, he realised that the automatic emergency sprinklers had done their job. Downstairs the fire had been too widespread, but up here in the smaller rooms the flames had been contained and snuffed out.

The Doctor stepped into the room where he'd met Uncle and crossed the sodden carpet. Looking up, he noticed something attached to one of the light fittings. Pulling the sonic screwdriver from his jacket pocket, he fired a blast of sound into the air. The little black box fell into his outstretched hand.

'Ouch!' It was still hot. The Doctor dropped it and it continued to smoulder on the carpet. He quickly adjusted the screwdriver's settings and gave the box another dose. This time the little firebomb behaved itself and shut down.

The Doctor bent down to examine it. There was something familiar about the design of the unit, something he knew he should recognise, but for the moment it eluded him.

He heard movement in the corridor and remembered that he was here looking for someone. He ran out into the corridor and caught a glimpse of white clothing disappearing around the corner.

'Wait!' he cried and ran after the figure.

A moment later he reached the lifts, where the figure was revealed to be Uncle's daughter. She was stabbing a finger at the lift controls with determination and little patience. She was coughing a little but other than that she seemed unhurt.

'I don't think the lifts are working right now.'

Hope jumped at the sound of his voice.

'What are you doing here, creeping around?' she complained. 'You nearly gave me a heart attack.'

'Sorry,' the Doctor apologised, 'I didn't mean to scare you. In fact I came to, well, rescue you. From the fire…'

'A knight in shining armour!' she smiled.

'More of a brown suit, really, but I suppose beggars can't be choosers,' replied the Doctor, returning her smile.

'I found this in my room,' Hope continued, showing him something she had in her hand. The Doctor realised that it was the control device they'd found earlier.

'Let me see,' he murmured, holding his hand out. She passed it over and he took a closer look.

Looking at it again the Doctor made the connection to the similar box he'd just found in Uncle's meeting room – the firebomb that had started the conflagration. They were of the same design, a linked pair. A firebomb and a detonation device.

'Do you know what it is?' Hope wondered.

The Doctor nodded, as he led Hope towards the stairs. 'It's the signal device that just set off these firebombs.'

'Firebombs!' she exclaimed, looking around fearfully.

'It's OK,' he reassured her. 'It's all under control.'

'How many bombs were there?' she asked, nervously.

'There was at least one more, downstairs, but it's been dealt with.' He produced the sonic screwdriver and zapped the control box. 'And now if there are any more hidden around here they won't go off,' he assured her.

He led her towards the stairs. 'Where did you say you found this?' he asked her as they walked.

'Back there,' Hope told him, waving rather imprecisely back towards her room. 'I saw someone drop it.'

'Really?'

Hope nodded vigorously. 'Is it a clue? Will it help catch whoever did this?' she asked hopefully.

The Doctor just shrugged. 'You never know,' he told her. 'So tell me what you saw.'

'There was a man, he was lurking in my room, doing something with that box. When he saw me, he dropped it, pushed past me and ran off. Not long after that the fire alarms went off,' she recalled.

'And would you recognise the man again?' wondered the Doctor.

Hope stopped and looked at him with wide eyes. 'Of course I would. He had blue skin!'

***

Uncle was overjoyed when the Doctor emerged from the still-smoking Casino with Hope. The anger was all gone now, replaced with a deep gratitude. The Doctor felt a little uncomfortable, but realised that it might be useful to be owed a favour by such a powerful man.

'How can I ever thank you?' Uncle asked him.

The Doctor paused. 'I'll let you know,' he told the crime lord and moved off towards the Judoon who was standing nearby with Nikki. She'd obviously managed to retrieve her own clothes and had got rid of the Casino uniform. She was now deep in conversation with the Judoon Commander, comparing notes.

'This girl has information that might aid us,' the Judoon announced as the Doctor joined them.

'Looks like the case I'm working is linked to your exploding man thing,' Nikki said brightly. 'Maybe we can help each other out?'

'I thought private detectives liked to work alone?' the Doctor observed.

'Not me,' Nikki replied. 'I prefer to work in a team. Usually I'm partnering Dad. It's his detective agency.'

'Then we will work with your father,' rumbled the Judoon. 'This is dangerous work for a young female.'

'What's with the dinosaur here?' retorted Nikki, affronted. 'For your information, my dad's on another case right now, so it's me or nothing.'

The Doctor stepped between them. 'I'm sure we can all work together,' he told them, grinning. 'Three heads are better than one. And my head's gotta be worth more than one on its own. So that's at least four...'

'Doctor!' the Judoon interrupted him. 'Just tell us what happened with Uncle's daughter. Did you find anything else in there?'

The Doctor frowned. 'I'm not sure,' he confessed and told his new partners about the conversation he had just had with Uncle's daughter.

'The prime suspect for these firebombs appears to be this blue-skinned man,' the Judoon Commander stated.

Nikki shook her head. 'No, that's not right,' she insisted. 'Deselup's a pickpocket, not an arsonist. And anyway I followed him here tonight – he didn't have any bombs with him then, I'm sure of it.'

The Doctor pulled a face. 'I suppose Hope must have been mistaken about what she saw.'

'We'll just have to track Deselup down and ask him ourselves,' Nikki suggested.

The Doctor was deep in thought. The Walinski brothers had been at the spaceport for a reason, he was sure about it. The exploding man had been killed, but that couldn't have been their prime mission. No, they must have been there for something else. Something the man who'd died was meant to give them.

'But he didn't give it to them because he didn't have it!' the Doctor concluded his analysis out loud. Nikki and the Judoon Commander just looked at him as if he was mad. Quickly the Doctor outlined his theory.

'The man who died was meant to deliver something to the Walinski brothers,' explained the Doctor. 'Probably something to do with that Invisible Assassin. But when the moment came he couldn't deliver the, well, whatever it is.'

'Because ol' Deselup had taken it from his pocket,' Nikki concluded, following the Doctor's thinking. 'No wonder he was nervous,' she added.

The Doctor nodded. 'That's why he was here – to try and do a deal on the whatever it is that he purloined from the man who died. He must have seen the Walinski brothers with the victim at the spaceport and put two and two together.'

'We need to speak to this pickpocket,' the Judoon rumbled. 'How are we going to find him?'

'Oh that's no problem,' announced Nikki holding up her wrist-puter. 'I planted a tracker on him,' she told them proudly, 'so wherever he is in the city, I can find him. Shall we go?'

NINE

It was raining again, a light persistent rain that entirely failed to make the city feel any cleaner. The dark shadows remained and, as the mismatched trio of investigators walked along the streets, they were aware of suspicious glances coming their way from all directions. It was a hostile environment, where passers-by dropped their heads and hurried along without making eye contact with any stranger. As they walked, Nikki filled in the Doctor and the Judoon Commander about the recent history of the city.

'It's a mess,' she confessed. 'It sort of grew without proper planning so it's a real mixture of styles, all sorts of buildings all jammed on top of each other.'

'According to our scans ninety-eight per cent of the planetary surface is undeveloped,' the Judoon told them.

'That's cos no one's interested in the planet itself,' Nikki pointed out. 'All this,' she waved at the city around her, 'all this is here because of the spaceport. That's why it's crammed in.'

'So who's this Widow woman, then?' asked the Doctor, recalling Uncle's reaction to the incendiaries.

'A place like this is a breeding ground for crime. That's what Dad says anyway.' Nikki grinned. 'Good for those of us in the private investigation business but tough on the city sometimes. It's like there's two cities in one, really. There's the legal one, with the City Council and the Police Service and the Spaceport Authority, and then there's a whole other world, an underground. And that's ruled by the criminal gangs.'

Nikki explained that Uncle had been the kingpin in the city for as long as anyone could remember. 'Apparently, he started out on the street but worked his way up the criminal ladder. Eventually, he killed the previous gang leader and took over. Since then he's ruled with an iron fist. Nothing criminal goes on without Uncle's organisation knowing about it. The joke around here is that his gang is more efficient than the City Council!'

'That is anarchy,' complained the Judoon. 'Lawbreakers should face justice.'

'Yeah, well, if we had an army of blokes like you, maybe they would,' replied Nikki.

'Don't even think about it!' warned the Doctor.

The Judoon shook his massive head. 'This is outside my jurisdiction. My only concern is to apprehend the Invisible Assassin.'

'And when we catch up with our light-fingered blue-skinned friend we'll be a step closer to achieving that,' promised the Doctor.

'Trouble is, Uncle's not the man he used to be,' Nikki continued her explanation. 'There's a new organisation in town. They're called the Widow's Gang. About eighteen months ago, this mystery woman appeared on the scene, linking up some of the minor gangs into a super-gang powerful enough to take on Uncle. She took advantage of the fact that Uncle had put a lot of noses out of joint over the years.'

'Is that literally or metaphorically?' wondered the Doctor.

'Both. Let's face it, in Uncle's line of work you're going to make enemies. But until the Widow came along, all his enemies hated each other as much as they hated him, if not more. The Widow changed that. She made them see their antipathy towards Uncle as common ground and she built on that.'

'But who is this Widow?' demanded the Judoon Commander.

Nikki shrugged. 'That's the thing. No one knows anything save her name – Madame Yilonda. She's a mystery. She just appeared out of nowhere. Even after eighteen months, there's no more information about her, not even what she looks like. For all we know, she could be an alien like you!' Nikki looked at the Judoon again and shook her head. 'Maybe not like you,' she corrected herself.

'Someone must know something,' the Doctor pointed out.

'Well if they do, they're not saying.' Nikki was looking at her wrist-puter. 'Deselup's stopped moving,' she announced.

'So where is he?' the Judoon Commander asked.

'In there!' she said triumphantly. She pointed to a brightly lit building across the road. 'I should have known,' she added.

'Why?' asked the Doctor.

'Because the Spa is where everyone says you'll find the Widow's Web.'

The Doctor nodded and shot a look at the Judoon.

'Fancy a sauna? It'll do wonders for your skin!'

Inside the Spa, the blue-skinned man was looking around nervously. Deselup was a loner, used to keeping away from the gangs as much as possible. His only real contacts with the wider criminal community were the fences who transformed the valuable items he acquired into hard cash. The gangs were dangerous territory, full of paranoia, suspicion and double-dealing; Deselup had always kept well clear of it all.

The incident at the spaceport had changed all that. He'd seen the newsfeeds' coverage of the mysterious death, and when they had flashed an image of the dead man on screen his memory flashed too. He had always had a good memory for faces and he recognised the man instantly. He had been one of his victims this morning at the spaceport. He had taken a left-luggage reclaim chip from him, but with the chaos at the spaceport this morning he had not had the chance to discover what treasure had been left in the locker by the now deceased visitor. Seeing what had happened to the man himself, he wasn't entirely sure now that he wanted to know. But someone would, he was sure. The presence of the Walinski brothers suggested that Uncle might have an interest so, having made sure the chip itself was secure, Deselup had ventured into Uncle's domain to see if he could secure a price for the chip.

Uncle, however, had treated him like dirt, which annoyed the pickpocket. He might only be a street thief in Uncle's eyes, but there was no excuse for dismissing him so casually. He'd been asked to wait, while more important visitors were entertained. At first he had accepted it, but the longer he had waited the more the anger at his treatment had built. Finally he had snapped. Uncle could rot. There were other people in town who might pay for the chip, of that he was sure. For a start there was the Widow. She'd sent that girl to tail him earlier, hadn't she? The Widow would pay good money for the chip and whatever it would give access to in that locker. Terminal 13 might be in complete lockdown at the moment, but eventually things would return to normal and the Widow could then use the reclaim chip to pick up the prize – whatever it was! Confident that the Widow would pay handsomely where Uncle had failed, he had headed directly to the Spa, with a grin on his face.

That had been before he had been admitted to the Widow's base itself. Situated in basement levels below the Spa, it was a dark and creepy place, a location lacking in atmosphere that instantly drained him of every vestige of the confidence he had been feeling.

In one of the early expansions of the city, there had been a fledgling underground train system, now long abandoned and, for the most part, forgotten. Here in one of the old stations the Widow had made her nest. She shared her domain with rats, cockroaches and spiders and kept the place in semi-darkness.

Deselup shivered as a something scuttled and squeaked in the shadows.

'Don't worry,' a sultry voice surprised him, 'we keep them well fed.'

Deselup spun round as a figure stepped forward from the darkness. It was a woman. She was dressed in a figure-hugging, low-cut black dress that emphasised every curve of her perfectly proportioned body, and she had a neat black bob of hair framing a ghostly pale face. Her lipstick was a vivid, dark shade of red, and her eyes were all but concealed behind huge blue-tinged shades.

'I have something you might be interested in,' he told the woman, coming directly to the point.

The woman looked him up and down coolly. 'Really? You surprise me,' she told him.

'I don't know exactly what it is,' he continued, 'but it must be worth a small fortune.'

The woman said nothing. Deselup started to sweat, despite the cool temperature in this underground lair.

'Whatever it is, Uncle wants it,' he stammered, playing his trump card.

To his relief it worked. The mention of Uncle's name had an immediate effect on the Widow. She took a step closer and stood next to him, laying an arm across his shoulder.

'Why didn't you say so to start with?' she asked him, in a friendlier tone. 'Tell me more…'

The Spa was a place of peace and relaxation, its one purpose to be an oasis of calm spirituality in the beating heart of the naked city. It was a place designed to be a haven where the harsh realities of life in New Memphis could be forgotten. It was not a venue where violence was either expected or welcome. It was therefore not prepared in any way, shape or form for the arrival of a Judoon Commander, brandishing a weapon in each hand and crashing, literally, through the double glass doors leading to the reception atrium.

The Judoon Commander, following the Doctor's suggestion to the letter, flicked off his translation unit and barked at the terrified customers in his native tongue.

'Ra, Ho, Bo, No, Ho-So, Ro,' he intoned, each clipped syllable emerging like a bullet from a rapid-firing machine gun.

The clientele at the Spa were terrified. The Judoon reactivated his translation unit and addressed the cowering humans who trembled in front of him.

'Under Galactic Law, I order that you give up the entity known as Horat Deselup,' he intoned gravely.

One man, dressed in a fluffy towelling gown and wearing thick-soled flip-flops, managed to find his voice. 'I think you might be in the wrong building,' he stammered. Then, as an afterthought, he added, 'Sir.'

Outside the Spa entrance, the Doctor and Nikki waited in the shadows.

'How long do we give him?' asked Nikki.

'I reckon he'll have made an impact by now,' suggested the Doctor. 'Follow me.' He led the way into the building.

As they expected, everyone in the foyer was looking in the direction of the Judoon, who was now barking out a long list of what Nikki presumed were genuine galactic laws that the Spa clients and management were in danger of breaking. The Doctor nodded at the damage that the Judoon had caused when he had made his entrance. Amongst the rubble of what had been the doorway, Nikki could see that the Judoon had cleverly managed to take out the security camera that would normally record the image of all visitors. Keeping close to the wall, and making sure everyone continued to be occupied by the antics of the Judoon Commander, the Doctor and Nikki reached the lifts. The floor indicator showed only three floors above, but the Doctor applied the sonic screwdriver and soon had access to the hidden lower levels. The doors of the lift slid open, and the Doctor and Nikki jumped inside, confident that no one had noticed them.

The doors of the lift opened again to reveal the dark and dusty old underground station. 'Just like the old White City,' the Doctor muttered to himself with a grin. 'I love old railway stations. Never know what you're going to find in them. Blokes worshipping old books and fighting over water, giant robotic yeti. Of course, sometimes it's just men with guns...' His voice trailed off.

'What sort of guns?' asked Nikki, who was walking behind him and cannoned into his back when he stopped suddenly.

'Those sort of guns,' said the Doctor and stepped to one side to show Nikki the man standing in front of them holding a massive gun in each hand.

The man was not tall, but what he lacked in height he made up for in width. He was very large and managed to make his smart suit look as if it had been purchased for a man half his size. His puffy face was impassive, with blunt features and no hair. His eyes were invisible, hidden behind trendy shades.

When he spoke, it was in a surprisingly quiet voice that was almost a whisper, but there was nothing gentle about it. It was a deathly voice, a gravelly, husky voice that made every utterance sound like a threat. 'The Widow will see you now,' he said simply and jerked the guns in the direction he wanted them to move.

The giant gunman herded Nikki and the Doctor into a room where the Widow was waiting perched, cross-legged on an incongruous leather sofa.

'I am Madame Yilonda,' she introduced herself, without moving from her semi-prone position, 'and I don't like people sneaking around my property.'

Nikki stepped forward. 'We didn't want to bother you, we know you're busy. We're just looking for someone.'

'And who would that be?' the woman asked, shifting lightly on the sofa and making her curves even more obvious. Nikki glanced at the Doctor but he didn't seem to have noticed.

'A man called Deselup. A pickpocket. Blue-skinned?' answered Nikki, making her last response more of a question in intonation.

'Never seen the man,' the Widow told her firmly. 'Now I suggest you turn around and leave my premises before I decide to turn my new bodyguard here on you. He assures me that he is capable of killing a man in ninety-six different ways with his bare hands, and he's a bit out of practice.'

'Bit out of shape more like,' Nikki joked cheekily.

With a grunt, the bodyguard took a step closer to Nikki, but for some reason she didn't feel scared. Although he looked fearsome, some instinct was telling Nikki that he was a pussycat inside.

'Taron, no,' ordered the Widow, and the massive figure of the bodyguard took up his former position.

Nikki frowned. The name Taron sounded familiar but she couldn't place it.

Before she could give it any further thought, she noticed the Doctor bounding forward towards the Widow. He extended his hand to shake hers.

'So sorry to bother you,' he was saying, 'but it's lovely to meet you.'

Taken by surprise, the Widow allowed him to take her hand, but to her astonishment he didn't shake it but bent to kiss it. He looked up at her and gave her a wink. 'Thanks for your time!'

Finally, he released her hand and stepped back, almost stepping on Taron's toes. The Doctor glanced over his shoulder and then back at the Widow.

'We'll be going now, then,' he said quickly, stepping round the bulky bodyguard and bundling Nikki back the way they had come. 'No need to show us out.'

***

Deselup was sweating again. *Why did things keep going wrong for him? Why couldn't a man make a dishonest buck without all these problems all the time?* Just when he thought things were going well with the Widow, there had been some commotion in the Spa above and the meeting was abandoned. The Widow's fat bodyguard had appeared and escorted him to a waiting area and, once again, the blue-skinned man had been sidelined.

Deselup got to his feet. He was sick of being treated like this. He left the waiting area and went in search of an exit. If this Spa had been built over the ruins of the old subway station, there had to be stairs somewhere heading back to the surface. Eventually he found what he was looking for and, after a short climb, he emerged into one of the private areas of the Spa. It was strangely depopulated. *Had the Spa closed? Was it that late?* A moment later, the reason became clear. Standing in the foyer of the Spa was a massive alien clad in leather battle armour and carrying a vicious-looking weapon. His grey skin was wrinkled and mottled and his long snout was topped by two gleaming horns. Two tiny eyes burnt with a black intensity either side of the second horn, and on top of his head two strangely small ears could be seen. The alien opened his mouth to reveal huge yellowing teeth. Even from here the fetid smell that emerged from that mouth made the pickpocket gag.

In a day that had been far from one of his best already, this was a new low. It was the most terrifying sight he had ever seen but it was about to get even worse. The creature turned his head towards him and the tiny eyes locked on his own. The alien raised his arm and cried out but Deselup didn't wait to hear what the nightmare had to say to him. Instead he bolted, crashing through the remains of the door and disappearing into the night. He ran as if his life depended on it, and he didn't once look back.

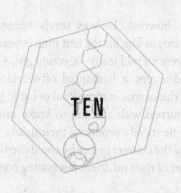

TEN

The all-night café that they found in a street around the corner from the Spa was a popular haunt for shift workers and anyone else who slept during daylight and worked through the night.

Carlos the proprietor prided himself on a strict no-questions-asked rule when it came to his punters. His café had been the location for all sorts of assignations – for cheating husbands, assassin-briefing wives, last-minute negotiations, hard-bargained deals and betrayals both professional and personal. Carlos just took the punters' money, provided them with the food and drink they ordered and let them conduct their business – whatever it was – without interference or comment. If asked, he never, ever remembered a face, let alone a name or a fragment of conversation. His cultivated lack of interest was a vital skill and kept him safe in a dangerous world.

Tonight, however, he was sorely tempted. Tonight curiosity flared in him for the first time in years. The three strangers were an odd team – a young girl, a local by her clothes and accent, a humanoid off-worlder with busy eyes, and a rhinoceros in some kind of battle garb.

Carlos burned with a desire to know more but, true to himself, he merely produced their drinks and hurried back behind the counter before he could even overhear the merest sliver of their no doubt fascinating conversation.

The Doctor watched the café owner as he walked back behind his counter. When he was sure that the man was out of earshot, he spoke to his friends.

'Not going too well, is it?' he whispered.

'I am sorry,' rumbled the Judoon Commander. 'I was not fast enough to catch our quarry.'

'Never mind, big guy,' said Nikki sympathetically. 'We've still got my tracker. We can find him.'

'And he'll run again,' complained the Judoon. 'Let me bring my men down. With a thousand Judoon on the streets we'll soon corner him.'

The Doctor shook his head. 'It will cause a riot. Haven't you learnt anything yet? Sometimes less is more.'

'Less effective. Less successful. Less efficient. Less Justice,' intoned the Judoon and then made a noise that sounded like a tumble dryer starting up. It was only when Nikki saw the alien's shoulders were shaking that she realised he was laughing. She winked at the Doctor, warming to the alien. He might be big and scary, but he had a sense of humour and was able to laugh at himself.

'You know, maybe we're going about this the wrong way,' suggested the Doctor.

'You can say that again, hey Jude?' Nikki said cheekily, nudging the arm of the alien.

'No, I'm serious. If we think our blue-skinned friend took something from the man at the airport, something he thinks is valuable, why would he have it on him?' the Doctor pointed out.

'You're right,' agreed Nikki. 'He wouldn't walk about with the merchandise while trying to negotiate a deal. Not with the people he was trying to deal with. That'd be suicide.'

'No honour amongst thieves,' added the Doctor.

'There is never honour in theft,' proclaimed the Judoon Commander, but Nikki could now recognise the twinkle in the eye that indicated a degree of irony in his words.

'So where would a man like that hide something valuable?'

'Well, we could start with his home,' suggested Nikki, 'but we don't know where he lives.'

'Somebody must. We know his name. Let's call our friends at Police HQ.'

The Doctor borrowed Nikki's communicator and placed a call to Detective Corilli's office. Corilli herself was unavailable, but Dantin was able to give them the information they needed. The Doctor thanked the scruffy detective for his assistance and ended the call. He handed the phone back to Nikki, but the Judoon Commander reached out to take it from him. He quickly jabbed at the controls and then passed it to Nikki.

'What did you do?' she asked, taking the communicator back.

'Installed Judoon contact frequencies,' he answered. 'If we become separated, you will be able to contact me or my men.'

Nikki grinned. 'Cheers, Jude, that's brilliant.'

The Doctor got to his feet. 'Come on then, let's get going,' he suggested.

'Service is swift,' the Judoon Commander told Carlos as he left a large tip on the table. 'Thank you.'

Uncle was not at all happy, and he wanted the Walinski brothers to share his pain.

'How could this happen?' he demanded, as he paced in front of the brothers. 'An incendiary bomb attack on my headquarters, on my private apartments! This is a step too far!'

Wisely, the brothers said nothing, allowing Uncle to continue venting his fury without interruption.

'This has to be the work of that Widow woman, whoever she is,' he declared, coming to a halt and eyeballing both men.

'If you two hadn't failed to pick up the Invisible Assassin at the spaceport, then this might never have happened!'

Again, the Walinski brothers chose to remain silent, rather than make any effort to explain their actions.

Uncle stopped pacing, coming to a decision. 'We must finish this, and soon. We can't let her get away with this.'

'We could retaliate in kind,' suggested one of the brothers finally.

'Raze that Spa place of hers to the ground?' continued the other.

Uncle shook his head. 'We don't need anything so crude. Let the Invisible Assassin do his work.'

The brothers kept their eyes firmly fixed on the floor, both aware of their failure at the airport.

'The Courier was telling the truth; he did not have the reclaim chip. I had our people at the City Morgue check his personal effects,' said Uncle. He shot a withering look at them both. 'It might have been a good idea to have looked for it yourselves before going ahead and killing him.' He activated a viewscreen and showed the brothers a clip taken from a security camera earlier that evening. It showed the blue-skinned man arriving at the Casino.

'His name's Horat Deselup,' Uncle told them. 'He was here just before the explosions. Said he wanted to talk to me about some business. Apparently he had something he was certain I'd be interested in acquiring.'

The brothers exchanged a quick look with each other. It did not go unnoticed by Uncle.

'My thoughts exactly. So I did some checking. Turns out this Deselup is a pickpocket, who often works at the spaceport…'

Uncle paused, hoping for a response, but the brothers just stood like robots waiting for further instructions. Robot henchmen, he sometimes thought, might have been a better idea.

'Find him. Get that reclaim chip,' ordered Uncle, 'and make sure he knows how grateful we are to him for looking after it.'

The brothers nodded curtly and withdrew.

The Doctor had persuaded the Judoon Commander that it was unnecessary to call one of his ships into range in order to teleport them across the city. Instead they had taken a cab. This proved to be a costly mistake when the Judoon managed to rip a massive tear in the roof of the vehicle with his horns when trying to squeeze into the rear compartment, but the instant admission of responsibility and the promise of full and speedy compensation pacified the angry off-worlder taxi driver, and they were able to complete their journey. It wasn't stylish, or particularly comfortable, but it didn't take too long in the end.

'There it is,' said Nikki, pointing as she hopped out of the cab. The cabbie had pulled over a few metres past the junction of 12th and Main, and the target building was a little bit further back on the actual corner. It was a large apartment block, with narrow ledges circling the building at five-storey intervals. There was a small unimpressive entrance at street level leading to the lifts which gave access to the thirty storeys above.

'Most of the upper floors are commercial lets,' explained Nikki as the Doctor struggled to help the Judoon escape from the tiny space he'd not long managed to squeeze into. 'Our man's got an apartment on the fifth floor,' she added. 'Pickpocketing must be a lucrative business,' she mused. 'This is a nice neighbourhood.

With a final effort, the Doctor managed to get enough momentum to pull the Judoon clear of the cab. He popped like a cork from a champagne bottle, knocking the Doctor off his feet and tearing a new gouge in the top of the door frame as he exited. Nikki looked back at them and raised an eyebrow.

'I thought we were meant to be inconspicuous,' she commented, but how that was a realistic prospect when you were accompanied by an unforgettable alien like the Judoon was, perhaps, a moot point. Nevertheless, despite his size and looks, the Judoon seemed to fit into the streets of New Memphis better than Nikki would have imagined. Perhaps it was something about his bulk and innate brutality that made him seem at home in this environment. Nikki realised with some surprise that she was beginning to like the giant alien.

'Sorry,' said the Doctor as the Judoon wordlessly helped him to his feet. Nikki grinned. The Doctor was easy to like, and he seemed to fit in everywhere and anywhere. But there was something secret about him, Nikki felt; a grief or a loneliness that he just couldn't quite keep hidden. She just knew instinctively that he was passing through and would soon move on from New Memphis, still looking for something he didn't even know he'd lost.

They managed to get access to the apartment with surprising ease. The Doctor used something he called psychic paper to persuade the security man at the door that they were inspectors from the health and safety department, and then Nikki had used her own special skills to pick the lock of the apartment they wanted to get into.

'Family business, remember. Dad says I was born picking locks,' she explained with a grin.

The Doctor and the Judoon exchanged a concerned look. Nikki had explained to them earlier about her father currently being missing, and both of them were worried at her slightly cavalier attitude to the situation. Nikki's voice trembled slightly as she said the word Dad, and for a moment she looked much younger than her years.

'Your father will return soon,' said the Judoon, laying a gentle, reassuring hand on her shoulder. She gave a brave smile and patted the Judoon's gloved hand, gratefully.

Beyond the door was a small hallway leading to an inner door. Nikki grabbed the handle confidently, pulled and nearly dislocated her shoulder. 'It's locked,' she announced, rubbing her shoulder.

They took turns to try and open the door but without success. It proved impervious to Nikki's lock-picking skills and immune to the Doctor's sonic device. 'Deadlock sealed,' he muttered to himself. Finally the Judoon made his attempt – brute force. He crashed into the door with his full weight, at speed, and only managed to bounce off and nearly crush the Doctor and Nikki.

'Somebody doesn't want any visitors,' the Doctor commented.

'Just have to try Plan B then,' grinned Nikki.

A few minutes later, Nikki was beginning to wonder if Plan B hadn't been adopted a little bit too quickly and that, perhaps, jumping on to Plan C or Plan D (which could have involved going home and sleeping) might have been a better option. Plan C had been quite good, too, involving getting the Judoon fleet back in range and using the teleport, but the time factor had made that a non-starter, so it was back to Plan B.

Unfortunately Plan B involved her inching her way along the narrow ledge that ran around the building below the window line. It was about twenty centimetres wide, just enough for her to stand on. Both the Judoon Commander and the Doctor had wanted to try but both were too big for the job; Nikki was their only hope. The idea was to creep along the ledge from another apartment on the same floor to the windows of the apartment behind the locked door. The theory being that the windows would be less well protected than the door.

With the wind whistling round her face and the sounds of the city below her, Nikki was seriously regretting her agreement to the plan.

'Another metre,' shouted the Doctor, encouragingly, leaning out of the window she had climbed through just a few minutes earlier. Behind him she could see the massive figure of the Judoon Commander holding tightly to the improvised safety rope. Without thinking about it consciously, Nikki checked the knotted sheets tied around her waist. The Doctor had assured her that he had been taught to tie knots by someone called Baden-Powell, which was meant to reassure her, but she couldn't help thinking that the most likely outcome if she happened to slip would be that the string of ripped sheets that her companions had made into a rope would just tear. With that thought in mind, she pressed herself harder back against the wall behind her and made another side step towards her goal. A few more vertiginous moments later and she reached the cool surface of the target window.

Now the tricky bit, she thought to herself. Carefully, she pulled the Doctor's sonic device from her pocket. He'd given her precise instructions and pre-set it, and all she had to do was press a small round control at the base of the rod. Nikki hadn't realised how cold her hands had become. Her fingers couldn't seem to grip properly, and she felt the device begin to slip from her grasp. Quickly, she brought her other hand round and caught the device before it could fall more than a few centimetres. But the action of swinging her arm around unbalanced her and she wobbled awkwardly for what felt like months. Finally, she regained her balance and leant back against the window. She carefully reached out to where the window lock was and applied the sonic device. To her great relief, she heard a pop as the mechanism released, and she was able to slide the window along and fall into the relative safety of the apartment.

Inside it was dark and, for a moment, Nikki just lay beneath the window where she had landed, grateful to be away from the risk of falling. As she lay there, her eyes adjusted to the low level of light and she could begin to make out her surroundings. Her heart sank as she took in the state the room was in. It was a mess. Someone had clearly beaten them to it. The room had been thoroughly ransacked with brutal efficiency. The intruders had meticulously taken the apartment apart, searching each and every corner of the room for something. Nikki got to her feet and looked around her – every cupboard, every drawer, every box had been pulled apart and checked. The apartment consisted of a living room with kitchen area, a bedroom and a bathroom. Nikki hesitated – should she rush to let the Doctor and the Judoon Commander in or should she take a look around first? It wouldn't take a moment just to check the other rooms, would it? If they were intact then they'd know the intruders had found what they were looking for.

Nikki pushed open the door of the bedroom and found a light switch on the wall just inside the room. She made the mistake of looking up towards the light fitting to check and, as it flashed into life, she was momentarily blinded. She blinked, and then froze. Across the room, either side of the bed, were two identical men. For a split second, Nikki thought her eyes were playing tricks on her, but then she recognised them and her heart almost stopped. The Walinski brothers.

Time seemed to stand still. The white-haired brothers looked at each other quickly. Some people believed they were mute, and there were whispers that the siblings had paranormal abilities. In fact, they were men of few words, and they certainly needed no words right now. With a curt nod, one of the brothers pressed a control on a wrist-mounted device and, without any further warning, Nikki was assaulted by a wave of sound. It was a high-pitched oscillating scream which seemed to penetrate to the very core of her being. It was like being attacked by a razor-wire-thin spike of frozen metal. Nikki clasped her hands to her ears but it was impossible to shut out the sound. Consciousness slipped away from Nikki as blood began to drip from her ears.

***

The Walinski brothers watched without any visible sign of emotion as the girl collapsed onto the floor, unconscious. The brother who had activated the weapon switched it off and they continued their search without giving her a second look. A few moments later, they left the room in a state of complete chaos. Clothes and possessions were spilt all over the floor, drawers were hanging out of units, their contents scattered to all four corners of the room. The brothers' search had been thorough but unsuccessful. Wordlessly, they left the room, stepping over Nikki's body as if it were just another piece of debris.

In the main room, the brothers stopped. Their search had been a failure, but they had not finished with the apartment yet. Moving with speed and efficiency, they set down the incendiary devices they had brought with them and primed each one. Then they released the deadlocked door and exited, shutting and resealing the door as they left.

Seconds later, the incendiary devices activated, exploding into small fireballs that instantly spread to the carpets and furniture. Within twenty seconds of the brothers' exit, the apartment was a raging inferno.

In the bedroom, Nikki began to stir. As she regained consciousness, she coughed, finding it difficult to breathe. She realised that she was surrounded by dense smoke. Quickly she got to her feet and pulled the bedroom door open. Beyond it she could see nothing except huge flames and more black smoke. She was trapped.

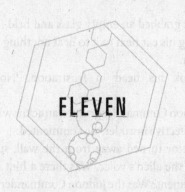

ELEVEN

The Doctor was worried. The Judoon Commander was no expert on humanoid body language, but even he could tell from his companion's relentless pacing that he was anxious about the girl.

The Doctor had not wanted to allow her to make this attempt to gain admittance to the apartment by such a dangerous route, but he had been outvoted. Nikki had insisted on going ahead, and the Judoon Commander had agreed that it was the logical thing to do. The Doctor had checked and rechecked the safety line that they had made from bed sheets, and only when he was certain that it would hold had he opened the window and let Nikki out onto the ledge.

There had been no sign of life since the tension in the line had been released as Nikki had tumbled through into the next door apartment and untied the sheets. The

Doctor had grabbed an empty glass and held it up to the wall, placing his ear next to it to hear anything that might be going on.

He shook his head in frustration. 'Nothing,' he reported.

The Judoon Commander grunted an acknowledgement. 'She is an effective intruder,' he commented.

The Doctor turned away from the wall, surprised at the tone in the alien's voice. Was there a hint of warmth in that statement? Was the Judoon Commander beginning to have some kind of emotional attachment to the young detective?

Perhaps he had misjudged the Judoon race, he pondered. He felt a little embarrassed to admit it, but it was very easy to tar an entire species with the same brush. *Bad move, Doctor,* he told himself, *you should know better.* If even clone races like Sontarans could have distinct personalities, then alien races like the Khellian Horde, the Hath and the Judoon were bound to be more varied. *After all,* the Doctor thought, *I've met Cybermen with personality and even Daleks with their own minds, why should the Judoon be any different?*

The Judoon Commander was looking at a handheld scanner, his eyes narrowing. 'Increased temperature,' he announced tensely.

'Heat?'

'Fire!' concluded the Judoon. And even as he was speaking an alarm began to sound.

'We have to get her out of there!' the Doctor yelled.

Without speaking, the Judoon marched across the room and reached out to touch the wall. He gave it a quick tap and then returned to his original position and lowered his head.

'You've got to be kidding me,' gasped the Doctor, but the Judoon Commander was entirely serious.

'Stand clear,' suggested the Judoon Commander and then, with a sudden burst of speed, he charged across the room, leading with the larger horn on his head. He crashed into and through the wall, sending plaster and brick fragments in every direction.

Immediately, thick black smoke poured into the room through the hole that the alien had just created. The Judoon pulled his head out and took a second run at the wall. This time he was able to enlarge the hole, and he plunged his entire body through the room into the smoke and flames beyond. Before the Doctor could join him, the Judoon was back, cradling a figure in his massive arms. Again without speaking, the Judoon ran straight past the Doctor and out of the apartment.

The Doctor finally caught up with the Judoon – and Nikki – outside the building. The Judoon, although he looked huge and ponderous, was actually capable of impressive bursts of speed. With Nikki in his arms, he had run at full speed to the emergency stairwell and then hurtled down, three, four steps at a time in an effort to get the girl to fresh air and safety. By the time the Doctor joined them in the street opposite the apartment building, the pair of them seemed to have recovered completely.

'I've never seen anything like it,' Nikki was laughing. 'Suddenly in the middle of the wall there was this great horn sticking out!'

'My father always told me to use my head,' the Judoon told her, his shoulders wobbling as he too laughed.

The Doctor felt a little bit left out. 'Are you OK, Nikki?' he asked. 'Smoke can do nasty things.'

Nikki explained that she'd soaked a piece of fabric in water, held it over her mouth and nose and kept close to the floor. 'That way most of the smoke was above me, and I avoided inhaling too much of it.'

The Judoon Commander caught the Doctor's eye. 'I told you this one was efficient,' he said, with more than a hint of pride.

The Doctor brought them back to reality and pointed out that the fire had destroyed their lead.

'It was the Walinski brothers,' Nikki told them. 'They were in the apartment when I got there.'

The Doctor nodded, taking the information in and adding it to everything else they'd seen. 'Time for a nice little bit of Hercule Poirot,' he announced to his baffled companions. 'Use the little grey cells. That Agatha Christie, she was brilliant!'

The Judoon Commander stared at the Doctor for a moment then turned back to Nikki. 'These brothers began the fire deliberately?' Nikki nodded. 'Then we must add arson and attempted murder to the charges when we arrest them,' concluded the Judoon. 'Justice—'

'*Should* be swift!' Nikki butted in. 'I can't argue with that – they did try and kill me. But you know what was most disturbing about it? It was so casual, like I was a bug or something tiny, an irritant.'

The Doctor was shaking his head. 'No, I don't think they

were trying to kill you at all. You were right – you weren't important enough to them.'

'Cheers,' replied Nikki, slightly miffed.

'No, listen,' continued the Doctor, 'that fire wasn't for you, it was to destroy the apartment. Think about it, use those little grey cells. Why would they want to do that?'

'To cover their tracks?' suggested Nikki.

'Why bother to do that, if they'd found what they were looking for?' The Doctor scratched his head, frustrated. 'No, that's not it,' he muttered, running things through in his head. 'Ah!' he announced suddenly. 'Then that must mean they *didn't* find what they were looking for.'

'Well if they didn't find it and we didn't find it…' Nikki began.

'… maybe it was never there,' finished the Judoon.

The Doctor looked at both his companions and nodded. 'Come on then,' he announced in an excited tone. 'We're still in the game!'

'But where are we going?'

'If our blue-skinned friend didn't hide whatever it is at home, he must have hidden it somewhere else, somewhere he knows pretty well.'

The Doctor began to walk away, heading back towards the heart of the city. The Judoon Commander fell into step beside him.

Nikki ran after them. 'So where are we going?' she demanded as she caught up.

'The Black Hole,' replied the Doctor, grinning. 'It's a bar.'

Nikki clicked her fingers. 'I know it. It's the bar where I

first found Deselup. But how do you know about that?'

The Doctor just smiled mysteriously and marched on.

Devoid of customers, silent and dark, the cavernous Black Hole bar was a very different place to the noisy, busy place it had been earlier in the night. Where earlier patrons had been jammed up against each other, now there was space. With the optics locked behind metal shutters, only the lingering smell of alcohol and smoke gave any clue as to the nature of the enterprise.

The Doctor had used his sonic screwdriver to disable the intruder alarms and Nikki had worked her lock-picking magic on a rear door. Now the three mismatched detectives were examining the interior with one thought at the front of their minds.

'Where would you hide something, in a place like this?' The Doctor vocalised the question they were all asking themselves. The Judoon upended the nearest table.

'Not here,' he answered, after checking the underside of the table for anything that might have been concealed there. He stepped towards the next table but the Doctor quickly moved in front of him.

'No, no, no,' insisted the Doctor. 'Let's be logical.'

The Judoon Commander exchanged a look with Nikki, who was already looking under tables herself. 'Go on then,' she prompted. 'Share that great brain with us mere mortals!'

The Doctor said nothing but started walking around the room. Suddenly he sat down and put his feet up on a table, resting his hands behind his head. 'We need to put ourselves in his head, see the world the way he does. That's the only way to get to what was he thinking…'

'He was thinking that he had something valuable that other people wanted,' offered the Judoon.

'And that holding on to it might prove dangerous,' added Nikki.

'Right,' agreed the Doctor, leaping up again. 'So what does he do? He's sitting here, drinking, looking around for a safe place to hide something.'

'How big is this something?' wondered the Judoon.

'Good question,' agreed the Doctor. 'Nikki?'

Nikki shrugged. 'Can't be that big if it was something he pickpocketed. Probably no bigger than a human palm. A coin, a key, something like that?'

She looked around the room carefully. Tables, booths, benches – lots of furniture but not many hiding places. The Doctor was walking towards the bar itself, a long wooden-topped counter with a number of stools aligned along it. He hopped up onto one of the stools and swivelled round. 'Whatever it is has got to be somewhere it won't be found by the wrong person,' suggested the Doctor, 'but somewhere that can be reached by the person who pays the right price for the information…'

The Doctor continued his spin, the stool now turning him away from Nikki and the Judoon Commander and back towards the bar. He stuck out an arm and knocked the charity box – a gaudy clown – which toppled and then fell.

The Doctor made no move to try and catch it as it tumbled towards the solid floor, where it smashed on impact, unleashing a wave of small change.

'Oops!' the Doctor muttered without a trace of contrition and slipped off the stool. Reaching down, he plunged his hand directly into the pile of coins and pulled out a small card with a glistening micro-chip on it. He held it up, grinning.

'What do we have here then?' he wondered, throwing it towards Nikki who caught it one-handed. She gave it a quick glance but she was already pretty sure she knew what it was.

'Access chip for a left-luggage locker at Terminal 13,' she announced cheerfully. 'Nice one, Doctor.'

The Judoon Commander came across and took the card from the girl. In his gloved hand, the device looked even smaller. 'Is this all there is?' he demanded. 'This is the prize?'

The Doctor shrugged. 'Not exactly, it's more of a key to the prize. The question is, what exactly will we find inside that locker?'

'You want to go and find out?' asked Nikki, enthusiastically.

The Doctor's eyes twinkled. 'Oh yes!' he replied, 'Shall we?'

'Wait!' It was the Judoon Commander. He looked troubled. 'We promised the local law authority that we would cooperate fully,' he reminded them.

The Doctor sighed. The Judoon was right, they had promised to keep Detective Corilli in the loop. After all, it had been Dantin's intelligence that had provided the Doctor with the address of the bar.

'Are you serious?' asked Nikki, incredulously. 'You think they'd go out of their way to help us? Why should we owe them anything?'

'Because they are the law,' insisted the Judoon.

Reluctantly, Nikki allowed her companions to persuade her, and she put a call through to Corilli. To her surprise, she got connected immediately. She flicked her communicator to loudspeaker so they could all hear and be heard.

'Looks like a left-luggage access chip from the spaceport,' Nikki explained, after telling Corilli how they had found it.

'Now all we have to do is to find the door that key opens,' added the Doctor.

'Wait there,' ordered the policewoman after a moment's consideration. 'I'll get over there and we'll go find out what this is all about.' She terminated the call.

'She could have said thank you,' Nikki complained.

'I'm sure she will when she gets here,' the Doctor told her.

Nikki shrugged and got to her feet. 'Yeah, well, I need some air. You guys may be doing all right, but I still need to find Mrs Kellingham's watch,' she reminded them.

She headed towards the exit, and the Judoon Commander instantly got to his feet to follow her. The Doctor stopped him with a swift shake of the head.

When the door stopped swinging behind Nikki, the Judoon turned to the Doctor.

'She's worrying about her father.' It was a statement rather than a question and it took the Doctor by surprise.

'Every time she looks at her communicator, you can see

the disappointment in her eyes,' the Judoon continued. 'She can't quite believe her father hasn't made more of an effort to contact her.'

'You may be right,' the Doctor agreed. 'You don't miss a trick, do you?'

'Justice must be vigilant,' the Judoon told him gravely.

'Keep 'em peeled,' said the Doctor with a wink.

The Judoon just looked at him blankly.

'You never seen *Police Five*?' asked the Doctor, his face falling. 'No?' He grinned. 'Oh well, don't worry – some things are beyond translation.'

They heard the door to the street bang open again. A moment later the interior door to the main bar swung open too. Nikki came through the door, but she was not alone. Immediately behind her came a brutal-looking thug, holding a weapon to her head. He pushed Nikki forward and came further into the room.

'No one move, no one gets hurt,' he told them as half a dozen other men entered behind him, all brandishing weapons. The Doctor instantly raised his hands and nodded to the Judoon to do the same. Two of the men quickly patted down the Doctor and the Judoon, removing the alien's weapons and the Doctor's sonic screwdriver.

'Sorry,' Nikki said, trying and failing to keep the fear out of her voice. 'They came out of nowhere. At first I thought it was Corilli—' she continued.

'But the good detective couldn't get away so she sent us,' a new but familiar voice concluded her sentence.

'Uncle!' said the Doctor as the crime lord joined his men in the bar.

Uncle was holding the reclaim chip in his hand. Nikki shot a look at the Doctor and mouthed a 'Sorry'.

'Thank you for tracking this down,' Uncle told him with more than a hint of irony. 'You've saved me a lot of bother.'

'Glad to be of service,' replied the Doctor sarcastically. 'Now would you mind asking your friend there to remove that blaster from the side of my friend's head?'

'I'm sorry, but that won't be possible just yet.' Uncle dusted down a chair and sat carefully. 'I need you to do me one more little errand before I can release the young lady.'

'Judoon do not run errands,' insisted the Judoon Commander in a low and threatening tone.

'Then it's time you started,' Uncle snapped back. 'I want you and the Doctor to go and collect the contents of the locker this key opens.'

He tossed the access chip card across the room and the Doctor caught it deftly with one hand while keeping his eyes on Uncle the entire time.

'With Terminal 13 still locked down, it's a little hard to get access at the moment,' Uncle continued, 'but I'm sure you two will find a way…'

The Doctor nodded curtly, accepting the mission.

'You will speak to no one about this, you will go directly to the spaceport and you will bring the contents of the locker to the Casino within six hours,' ordered Uncle simply.

'Or?' The Doctor raised an eyebrow. 'Just so I know.'

Uncle smiled coldly and got to his feet. 'Let's just say a promising career in the private detective business might be terminated tragically and prematurely.' He nodded at Nikki's captor, who responded by ushering their prisoner towards the door.

'Don't worry about me,' Nikki called out as she was manhandled out of the room.

Uncle's men started to move towards the exit, walking backwards and keeping their weapons pointed at the Doctor and the Judoon Commander at every stage. At the door, Uncle placed the Judoon blaster and the Doctor's sonic screwdriver on a small table.

'Six hours,' he repeated and then he was gone.

TWELVE

Jase Golightly was exhausted. It had been another long day at the office for him. Technically, it was already tomorrow and he had meetings lined up in just a few hours' time, but if he didn't at least make the effort to go home and try to sleep – even if it was only for an hour or two – then he'd never be ready. Golightly wanted a shower. He wanted something to eat. He wanted his bed. What he didn't want was to walk out of the main entrance to the spaceport and run into two of the aliens who had caused so much trouble earlier in the day.

'Mr Golightly! Just the man we wanted to see,' said the humanoid one, who had called himself the Doctor.

'We need access to the left-luggage areas,' said the rhino-headed one, in his familiar brusque manner.

A thousand answers ran through Golightly's head, from the mildly rude and sarcastic to the deeply offensive and aggressive, but in the end he merely muttered a resigned 'yes' and turned on his heels to lead his visitors back inside the spaceport.

'So is this something to do with the Invisible Assassin? What have you found out about the man who exploded?' he asked, his curiosity getting the better of him.

'We cannot say,' the Judoon Commander told him firmly.

'But… I need to know. The problems in Terminal 13, the disappearing luggage, you said you thought it was all connected. Please, I need to know what you've discovered.'

'I said we cannot tell you,' thundered the larger alien.

'But…'

The humanoid part of the duo turned to give him a sympathetic look and shook his head. 'Really, we can't tell you anything,' he said, in a kinder tone. 'Just take it from me that we will tell you everything you need to know when we're free to do so. But we are making progress, I promise you.'

Jase looked the man in the eyes and could see that he was being genuine. If he couldn't tell him any more details at the moment then there was a good reason for it, and he'd just have to accept that.

'OK, I can wait,' he agreed, 'but I will want a full explanation in time.'

'Good,' the Doctor cut in. 'Look, can we get on? We're on a bit of a short fuse and we need to get to those left-luggage lockers.'

A new figure suddenly appeared in the corridor ahead of

them. 'I'm sorry, but in matters of security I have ultimate authority,' said a familiar voice, 'and unless you can satisfy me as to what you are here for, you're not going anywhere near any lockers.'

General Moret stood in front of them, arms folded and his expression fixed.

'So, what's it going to be?'

Jase saw the Doctor and the larger alien exchange a look, but he couldn't decipher the meaning behind it. *Why were they being so secretive? What were they really here for? Perhaps,* Golightly began to wonder, *perhaps Moret was right to insist on some answers.*

If you are going to be taken prisoner and held as a hostage, thought Nikki, then her present experience was probably the best way to have it happen.

After the initial shock and discomfort of being grabbed from behind and having a gun pointed at her head had receded, her subsequent treatment had been much more agreeable. Uncle explained that she would be taken back to the Casino in his own car. With just one armed bodyguard to keep her in check, the journey was almost pleasant. Uncle's car was a luxury model with inertia dampeners that all but removed any sensation of movement. As they drove, Uncle engaged her in casual conversation, as if they had met across a dining table at a dinner party rather than as prisoner and captor. Uncle was intrigued at her involvement in her father's business.

'A real family business?' he said, in a tone that suggested both approval and a hint of jealousy.

'I guess so,' Nikki replied. 'I suppose I grew up seeing Dad at work and never thought about doing anything else.'

Uncle sighed. 'I sometimes wish I had a similar relationship with my daughter,' he confessed.

Nikki realised she couldn't really see Uncle as a father. 'What does your daughter think of the kind of work you do?' she asked him bluntly.

'She knows nothing of my work,' Uncle explained. 'She just knows that I am in business and that's all she needs to know. I want her to have nothing to do with this sordid world.'

'You don't want her to take over from you eventually?' Nikki asked.

'This isn't a business, girl, it's organised crime. It's dog eat dog. A matter of escalating violence and raw aggression. It's no way to live,' replied Uncle with surprising bitterness.

'So why do it?'

Uncle shrugged. 'It's all I know. But Hope lives in a different world, and I intend to keep it that way. I'm doing this for her so she has the choices and opportunities that I didn't.'

For a moment, Nikki almost felt sorry for the man. His choice of lifestyle, of career, had denied him the possibility of a full and proper father-daughter relationship, a special bond that she almost took for granted.

Unfortunately, this train of thought forced Nikki to confront, once again, the fact that her own father seemed to be missing. *Was it possible that he was in the same state as she was, captured by some criminal enemy, and unable to make contact?*

She tried to think back over the past few days and weeks to see if there was anything in her father's recent caseload that might explain his absence. Lost in her own thoughts, the conversation between her and Uncle died a natural death, and they spent the rest of the journey in silence.

She was locked in a room somewhere above the Casino gaming hall. She had access to a bathroom, water to drink and even some food but, despite all these niceties, she was still a prisoner. Outside the door, one of Uncle's men stood guard, with instructions, Uncle warned her, that she was to be shot on sight if she tried to escape. Nikki knew he wasn't joking, but escape was far from her mind. She wasn't even curious about the Doctor and the Judoon Commander and their progress at the spaceport.

The only thing running through Nikki's mind, as she lay on the couch in her well-appointed prison cell, was a single question.

Where are you, Dad?

'It's quite simple,' explained General Moret for the third time. 'Either you tell me what you're doing here or you can leave now.'

The Doctor sighed. The military mind, as ever, was an intractable beast. 'I'm asking you to trust me,' he said patiently.

'This is a matter of life and death,' proclaimed the Judoon, simply and bluntly.

'Really? Whose?' insisted the spaceport security chief.

'Yours – if you do not cooperate,' hissed the Judoon, any patience he had rapidly evaporating.

'Oh, that helps,' groaned the Doctor, putting out a restraining hand.

'You should listen to your friend,' sneered the General, 'I don't take kindly to threats.'

'It was not a threat,' insisted the Judoon. 'It was a promise.'

The General and the Judoon glared at each other for a long moment. Although one was nearly twice the height of the other, and one was totally human and one a humanoid alien with the head of a rhino, there was a definite similarity between them, as if one were a distorted funfair image of the other, thought Golightly before stepping smartly between them like a referee in a boxing match.

'Now, now, we're all on the same side,' he said in a voice about a hundred times brighter than he felt inside. 'Can't we work out a compromise?'

The Doctor agreed with this suggestion. 'We just need to locate the left-luggage locker that this access code opens,' he said holding up the tiny micro-chipped card, 'and then we need to take the contents.'

'Where to?' demanded the security chief.

'That's the bit I can't tell you,' the Doctor confessed. 'But whatever it is in that locker, people have died over it. We'll take it out of the locker and out of the spaceport. Whatever it is, it will have no further effect on anything happening here.' The Doctor looked the General in the eye and raised a quizzical eyebrow. 'That's your main concern, isn't it? The security of the spaceport and all those who use it?'

General Moret nodded. 'Of course it is.'

'So if you take us to the left luggage, we can get on with

making this spaceport a safer place.' The Doctor smiled, pleased with his diplomacy.

General Moret hesitated and then turned on his heel. 'Follow me,' he ordered and marched off.

The Doctor leant over to whisper up at the Judoon's ear. 'See. Wasn't so bad, was it?'

'We are not finished with the man yet,' commented the Judoon firmly.

The Doctor glanced over at Golightly, who raised his eyebrows in sympathy. 'Come on then,' Jase said. 'Let's get on with it. I was hoping to get some sleep before my working day starts again.'

'When's that, then?' asked the Doctor.

Golightly made a big deal of consulting his watch. 'In about four hours,' he sighed and began walking off after his security chief and the Judoon, who were already thirty metres away.

One thing Nikki did know about her father was that he wouldn't want her to waste time and effort thinking about him when she needed to look after herself. Right now she was a prisoner, and her friends were being coerced into something because she was being held hostage. She needed to do something to improve all their positions. She forced herself to move on from worrying about her father and started looking around the room with a new focus.

When she'd first been placed here she'd been distracted by the creature comforts, but now she was looking at it with more analytical eyes. She needed to escape and as quickly as possible. If Uncle did not have her as a hostage then the Doctor and the Judoon Commander would not need to do anything for him.

There were two doors in the room – the main door to the corridor, beyond which the guard stood ready to prevent any exit, and the door to the en suite bathroom. The bathroom itself offered no possibility of escape – there was a small basin, a toilet, a shower and a ventilation grille. Nikki took a quick look behind the grille, hoping that there might be a shaft of sufficient size for her to use, but the pipes were no wider than her arm and would have been a close fit for a rat let alone a young woman.

Nikki's next focus was the windows, but they were firmly locked shut. Nikki was privately quite relieved to discover this – she had no appetite for any more daredevil climbing around buildings tonight; one such adventure was enough for one evening. Having discounted the usual entrances and exits, she began to consider alternatives. The floor was covered with a thick carpet, but she managed to dislodge it at one corner of the room and pulled it back, revealing a solid floor below. No possibility of escape there, not without a drill of some kind.

If you can't go down, Nikki pondered, *perhaps you can go up*. The ceiling was tiled and, when she climbed on to a table to investigate it, she discovered that it was a suspended ceiling. The tiles lay on a thin steel framework. She pushed up at a tile and dislodged it, allowing her to see the metal frame more clearly. There looked to be about a metre of space above the ceiling, a perfect hiding place. There was only one question – would the metal framework bear her weight?

'Only one way to find out,' she muttered to herself and she jumped up, grabbing hold of the metal crossbar. To her delight, she found that it was quite solid and seemed to cope with her hanging from it without bending in the slightest. From there it was just a matter of swinging a leg up until she could hook one over another of the metal bars. Not for the first time today, she was grateful for all the encouragement her father had given her, not just to excel at the mental skills that a good detective needed but also to keep her body fit and agile. With the grace of a born gymnast, Nikki managed to get herself into the crawl space above the ceiling and was then able to replace the tiles to remove any evidence of her means of departure.

Once she was in the crawlspace, she made another discovery. The area of metal framework extended beyond the area of the room she had been kept in. Obviously at some point this floor of the building had been reworked to make smaller rooms where larger rooms had once been. Carefully she began to crawl across the framework, away from the room she had been held in.

Nikki pulled back a ceiling tile and found herself looking down on Uncle himself sat at a desk. Carefully, she replaced the tile, not wanting to make any sound that might make the crime lord look up.

She crawled on a little further, taking care not to let any of her limbs hang under the metal frame. It was a slow process but finally she reached a place where she could hear no sound from below. She lifted a tile and checked – no one there. Carefully she let herself hang down from the frame. Unfortunately there was no table so she had a bigger drop to contend with, but she braced herself, let go and landed perfectly.

She allowed herself a little grin. So far so good. The room she had entered was in semi-darkness and appeared to be some kind of storeroom. She went to the door and was delighted to discover that it was not locked. She opened it a crack and took a peak into the corridor beyond. All clear. Moving quietly and with great caution, she stepped out into the corridor and walked away.

The corridor curved around and eventually led to a pair of lifts. Nearby she could see a door leading to stairwell. Which to take – the stairs or one of the lifts? She hesitated and that proved to be her undoing. Without her noticing, the lift nearest to her was activated. Suddenly the doors started to open.

Nikki was caught, exposed in the area just in front of the lifts. The doors continued to open. Nikki stood frozen to the spot as the opening doors revealed the contents of the lift – two familiar and terrifying figures in matching dark suits. The Walinski brothers!

The brothers stepped quickly out of the lift, separating slightly so they could cut off her possible routes of escape to the left and to the right. Nikki backed up until she felt the wall behind her. The brothers closed in on her relentlessly.

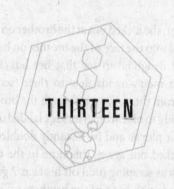

THIRTEEN

Nikki was trapped. With the brothers closing in on each side she had literally no place to run. There was no option but to fight. But these were Uncle's main enforcers – how could a teenage girl defeat the infamous Walinski brothers?

She flicked a glance at each brother in turn, looking for a hint of weakness, a clue as to where to attack first but there was nothing.

The two men were like mirror images of each other – even their slow relentless progress towards her seemed synchronised, like a practised ballet of looming danger. The twins were moving as one. Perhaps that was the weakness she was looking for?

Nikki felt along the wall for something she could use. Her hand reached a wall-mounted planter full of flowers and she grabbed a handful of the soil. Then, at exactly the same moment, she kicked out at the brother on her left and threw the soil into the face of the brother on her right.

Nikki was delighted to see that her hunch had been correct. Both men's hands flew to their faces to shield themselves from the soil, even though the brother on her left had nothing to hide from. Her kick landed undefended, in lefty's solar plexus and he instantly doubled up. Nikki spun and kicked out again, this time in the direction of righty, who was scraping mud off his face. Again her kick connected and, with both of the brothers off balance and distracted, Nikki dashed forward between them, towards the lift.

Suddenly her feet were running in mid-air as rock-steady hands grabbed her under the arms. Then she found herself jerked backwards and upwards before she crashed into the wall. She fell, dislodging the flower planter, which landed on her head. The brothers had recovered with incredible speed, and now it was Nikki who lay breathless and helpless while they advanced once more. For once, their usually blank faces were showing some sign of emotion: they were angry, furious. Nikki realised that she really was in a lot of trouble now. 'Never bother a wasp's nest,' her dad had always told her, but she'd well and truly put her foot in one this time.

The brothers loomed over her and, despite her determination to be resilient, Nikki couldn't help but squeeze her eyes closed. She waited for what seemed like an eternity, but nothing happened. Bravely she opened her eyes and found that time seemed to be standing still. The brothers were still hanging over her but they seemed somehow lifeless, like statues. Suddenly the pair of them keeled over, revealing another figure standing behind them, holding a stun gun in each hand. Nikki's eyes widened in surprise.

'You?!'

It was Taron, the bulky but dangerous bodyguard who worked for the Widow. *What was he doing here and why had he helped her?* Nikki swallowed hard. Things might just have gone from bad to worse.

The scale of the spaceport was impressive, even to the Doctor, who had seen his fair share of such places in his many lives. Much of the traffic that passed through was just that – passing traffic, stopping only for fuel and other supplies. Another major element of the spaceport's business was its function as a travel hub, a place where passengers and freight could transfer from one ship to another to continue a long-haul multi-operator journey. There were, therefore, extensive left-luggage storage facilities throughout the spaceport, including four within Terminal 13 itself. The Doctor was worried that they might have to check each one in turn. Golightly was able to reassure him.

'Each chip has a unique identification code,' he explained, 'so we can track down the locker associated with this card without any trouble.'

'And here we are, gentlemen,' announced General Moret as he led them into another huge warehouse. As they entered, the automatic systems reacted to their presence and low-level lighting came on, revealing the true extent of the space they had entered. The Doctor thought the room was probably the size of a football pitch, about the same size as the swimming pool he'd once had in the TARDIS, and it was full of long lines of metallic lockers, in horizontal and vertical rows.

The security officer passed the access code card through a reader, and a distant locker instantly lit up. Without a word, the Judoon Commander reached over and took the card from the reader and began to march in the direction of the spotlighted locker. The Doctor hurried to follow him.

'So some time yesterday the man who exploded must have come in here and deposited something in that locker, is that right?' asked Golightly, trying to keep up with events.

'That's what we think,' agreed the Doctor. 'Something of value that Uncle was expecting to have the Walinski brothers collect for him.'

'But they never got the chip card from him?'

'No. But we managed to track it down, so now maybe we'll find out why that man was murdered,' said the Doctor.

'And take it to the police, I guess?' Golightly persisted.

The Doctor hesitated. He didn't like to lie but at the same time he didn't want to risk anything happening to Nikki if he didn't follow Uncle's instructions to the letter.

The Judoon Commander thumped a locker in frustration, creating a diversion that enabled the Doctor to sidestep the awkward question.

'What's wrong now?' he asked the alien.

'It doesn't work,' snapped the Judoon Commander. 'The locker won't open.'

The Doctor could see that the Judoon was worried and angry – but not just about the locker. Like the Doctor, he had Nikki's safety at the forefront of his mind. The alien was clearly taking Nikki's predicament very closely to heart. They both knew that if they couldn't get the locker to open, Nikki's life would be in grave danger.

Nikki got to her feet, brushing soil and mud from her clothes and hair. The Widow's bodyguard just stood and watched her, his piggy little eyes almost invisible in the fat folds of flesh on his face.

'Thank you,' she said politely. 'Mind if I go now?'

Not entirely surprisingly, the man held up a hand.

'Yeah, I thought not. So what do you want from me?' Nikki retorted with more courage in her voice than she felt inside.

An unexpected emotion seemed to burn in Taron's eyes for a split second – was it amusement?

'Where are the others?' he rasped in his breathy sibilant whisper of a voice.

Nikki shrugged. 'Don't know who you mean!' she muttered.

'The Doctor and the other alien – the warrior – have they gone to the spaceport? Did you find the key?'

Nikki was surprised. How did the Widow's bodyguard know so much about what they were doing? Nikki realised that her thoughts were pretty transparent as Taron continued.

'Don't worry about how and what I know,' he hissed. 'Just answer my question. And be quick. That stun charge won't keep these boys quiet for long.'

Nikki considered her options. The man already seemed to know more than he should. Would it really make anything any worse to answer his questions?

'Yes, they've gone to the spaceport,' she confessed, hoping she was doing the right thing.

'And they have the key? The access code?'

'Yes, they have everything. Whatever that man was carrying, they'll be collecting any time now.'

The widow's bodyguard nodded and considered the information for a moment. Nikki decided to try and ask a question of her own.

'I guess the Widow wants a piece of that herself, is that why you're asking?' she wondered.

Taron shook his head gravely. 'She may already have her hands on it.'

'What do you mean?'

'It doesn't matter,' Taron insisted.

'It matters to me. My friends have gone to get this whatever it is, and you think your boss is going to get it herself? I don't like the sound of that,' fumed Nikki, getting angry.

Again Taron held out a pacifying hand to her, like a parent trying to get a whining child to be quiet.

'I know you've no reason to do this, but trust me. It's complicated. Very complicated. But if you trust me, no one will get hurt,' Taron whispered hoarsely, looking deep into Nikki's furious eyes.

'Trust you? You're the Widow's bodyguard. Why should I trust you?'

'Because things aren't always what they seem,' replied Taron. The Walinski brothers began to stir. 'They'll be awake in a minute. Find somewhere to hide. You'll do more for your friends here than elsewhere. Now move.'

Again Nikki hesitated. Should she listen to this man or should she just take her chance to escape?

'Trust me, Nikki. You must trust me.' Taron repeated.

The Judoon Commander drove his fist into the door of the adjacent locker, and it caved in as if made of cardboard. Golightly's mouth dropped open at this demonstration of sheer power and strength.

'That's not going to help,' said the Doctor calmly.

'It made me feel better,' muttered the Judoon, once again displaying a hitherto rarely seen sense of humour.

'Wait!' Golightly stepped forward before any more damage to spaceport property was attempted. 'Let me try,' he suggested, reaching to take the access card from the Judoon's gloved hand. Fixing him with a glare, the Judoon handed over the tiny piece of plastic.

'Security at Terminal 13 is state of the art,' Golightly continued, 'and these cards have some user-defined elements that can be set when they are initialised.'

The Doctor frowned. 'So the user can prevent anyone else using the card?'

'No, that might be a step too far,' Golightly explained. 'But you can set a time limit, or restrict access to members of certain species.'

'But the man is dead,' pointed out the Judoon. 'How can we ask him about its settings now?'

Golightly gave the alien the smile of a stage magician about to perform the Indian Rope Trick. He pulled a similar-looking card from his jacket pocket. He then approached the locker with a card in each hand. First he swiped their key through the reader and then, confidently, he swiped his own key. Golightly stepped back and waited.

For a moment nothing happened, and the Doctor began to wonder if the Judoon's punishment of the adjacent locker might not have damaged the mechanisms of the one they were interested in. Then, with a soft click, the door of the locker unlocked and swung silently open.

'Are you telling me that we could have come to you in the beginning and you could have opened that locker?' rumbled the Judoon, fearing that they had spent precious time on a wild goose chase.

Golightly hurriedly reassured him. 'Well, I could have used my master key to open every locker, but that could have taken years,' he clarified. 'You needed that key to know which locker to open so you can recover your…'

He paused and bent to peer into the cavernous locker, which was about a metre square and about three metres deep. At first glance it seemed to be empty, but then the Doctor's eyes adjusted to the lack of light and he could make out a single rectangular shape, pushed right to the back of the space. Golightly dropped to his knees and reached in to retrieve the object.

'… suitcase,' he announced, as he emerged into the light once more, dragging with him a rather nondescript and distinctly plain suitcase of a classic if not old-fashioned design.

The four of them stood around the case and looked at it with a mixture of confusion and disbelief.

'This is the package? Just this?' demanded the Judoon, poking it with his foot.

'Careful, if this is the Invisible Assassin's luggage it could be booby-trapped,' warned the security officer, gently moving the Doctor and Golightly back from the case.

Carefully, Moret got to his knees and listened to the case. The Judoon Commander loomed over him, casting a dark shadow. Moret looked over his shoulder and glared at the alien.

'Would you mind stepping back – give me some space, not to mention light, to work in?'

With a grunt, which may or may not have been a yes, the Judoon Commander took a few steps back and joined the Doctor and Golightly. The Doctor instantly leaned towards the Judoon.

'Do you recall mentioning the Invisible Assassin to General Moret?' he whispered urgently, while keeping his eyes fixed on Moret who was now examining the case carefully and cautiously.

The Judoon Commander's eyes narrowed as the significance of the Doctor's question dawned on him.

Moret got to his feet, holding the suitcase in one hand.

'I think I should take this to a place of safety before anyone tries to open it,' he announced and began to walk towards the door. 'Give me an hour, and I'll let you know what I find,' he added.

The Doctor nodded at the Judoon who quickly moved to stand between Moret and the door.

'That's very kind of you,' said the Doctor evenly, 'but we can handle it from here.' He held a hand out to take the case but Moret stepped away from him and, suddenly, there was a weapon in his hand. The old soldier raised the weapon and aimed it directly at Golightly.

'No,' he insisted, 'that is not going to be possible.'

'Moret, what are you doing?' screamed Golightly, his eyes focused on the barrel of the gun pointing directly towards his heart.

'Taking this to my boss,' explained the ex-soldier. 'The Widow badly wants this, and what the Widow wants the Widow gets. Now, you two,' he gestured at the Doctor and the Judoon, 'get over here now or I'll shoot Mr Golightly.'

For a moment it looked as if the Judoon Commander would ignore the threat and charge at Moret himself, but the Doctor managed to catch his eye. Slowly the Judoon Commander and the Doctor moved away from the door.

'But why? Why are you doing this?' Golightly was wide-eyed, as much from confusion as from fear.

'Once a mercenary, always a mercenary,' explained Moret simply. 'Every man has his price.'

The General backed towards the exit, his eyes flicking between the three of them while maintaining his aim at Golightly's chest. At the door he paused.

'But you work for me, for the spaceport,' Golightly replied, still not understanding.

'Then you can consider this my resignation,' Moret told Golightly. Suddenly dropping the barrel of the weapon, he fired off a single shot in the direction of the general manager's leg. Golightly cried out in pain and fell, clutching his damaged limb. The Doctor and the Judoon Commander ran to his aid. When they glanced back at the door, Moret was gone.

The Doctor ran across to the door and pulled at the handle but without any success.

'Locked!' he reported turning back to the Judoon. 'How is he?'

The Judoon was examining Golightly, who had lost consciousness, blood pooling under his damaged leg. 'He needs medical attention urgently.'

The Doctor had his sonic screwdriver in his hands and made a renewed attempt to open the door, but the lock would not open.

'Oh, why is everything deadlocked sealed these days?' moaned the Doctor. 'We have to find another way out.'

The Judoon, now carrying the limp body of Golightly in his arms, stood up and looked around.

'That might take some time,' he pointed out grimly. 'And we do not have that luxury.'

Blood continued to drip relentlessly from the unconscious man's injury, like sand pouring through an hourglass. Time was running out.

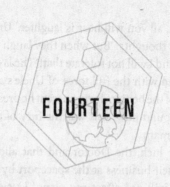

FOURTEEN

The Walinski brothers were standing in front of Uncle, unflinching, as he unleashed his fury upon them for the second time that day.

'What is the point,' he fumed, 'of holding a hostage and not knowing where she is?'

The brothers said nothing.

'And then you came across her and managed to let her elude you again! First the disaster at the spaceport, now this. What's happened to you? You've turned into a pair of clowns.'

For once, the impassive faces of the brothers revealed some emotion: their mouths tightened and they seemed to recoil at the accusation. Seeing the reaction, Uncle ploughed on.

'Yes – clowns! You're rapidly becoming a laughing stock. People used to be afraid of you – now when you enter a room, all you will hear is laughter.' Uncle paused, gathering his thoughts. 'But when they laugh at you, they laugh at me and I will not tolerate that!' The last few words were bellowed with the full force of Uncle's anger. There was no sign of the benign, loving parent he presented when Hope was around now; this was the fury of a dangerous and ruthless man.

'With any luck, the Doctor and that alien will have concluded their business at the spaceport by now, so the girl's escape will not affect my plans,' Uncle told them, calming down. 'When the Invisible Assassin strikes, we will regain our honour. No one will be laughing when the Widow and her whole pathetic organisation are wiped out for good.'

Nikki could not help but shiver as she heard the man talk so casually about taking so many lives. She had always known that the crime lords were cold and ruthless but had never really seen the extent of their evil first hand.

She was back in the crawlspace above the false ceilings of the rooms on this floor, perched above Uncle's office. She had lifted one ceiling tile just enough to watch and listen to the scene unfolding beneath her. Part of her wondered if she should have ignored the advice of the Widow's bodyguard and just escaped when she had the chance, but something about the way the stranger had spoken to her had convinced her to stay. As the brothers had begun to recover consciousness, Nikki had looked for a way to get back into the crawlspace. When she explained how she had escaped, the mysterious Taron had helped her climb back before disappearing himself. 'I was never here,' he told her with a peculiar grin, as if making a joke only he could understand, and then he was gone.

Now, lying here above Uncle's office, her thoughts once again turned to the stranger. *Why had he helped her? How had he got into Uncle's HQ with such ease? And who was he?* Nikki added it all to the list of questions being raised by this case and promised herself that she'd find answers to all of them in due course.

Below, Uncle seemed to have overcome his anger and was now smiling. Beaming, he sat back at his desk, put his feet up and threw his head back. Nikki froze, hoping he wouldn't spot the slightly out-of-place ceiling panel. For a long moment, she held her breath. *Was he looking up at the ceiling? Was he looking at her?* She closed her eyes, like a little child playing hide-and-seek, hoping that if she couldn't see him, he wouldn't be able to see her.

She heard something move and, despite her fear, opened her eyes. Uncle was no longer there. Nikki swallowed hard. *Was this it? Was she about to be discovered?*

Golightly was groaning, slipping between consciousness and unconsciousness with ever-increasing rapidity. The Doctor had made a temporary dressing with a strip of material torn from the poor man's own shirt, but the bleeding had hardly been staunched. The Doctor looked up at the Judoon who had been looking on at his first aid efforts with concern and interest.

'Any joy on an alternative exit?' he asked, more in hope than expectation.

The Judoon shook his head. 'Nothing.'

The Doctor laid Golightly gently on the ground, and made a makeshift support out of the manager's suit jacket. He got to his feet and began to look around. 'Take a look at that door and then look at these lockers,' he suggested. 'What do you notice?'

The Judoon shrugged. 'I do not know what you want me to say.'

The Doctor tapped the nearest locker, which made a satisfying hollow, metallic sound. 'These are solid,' explained the Doctor. 'Unless they were actually built here, which I doubt, each of these lockers was brought into this room. But not through that door – it's not wide enough. So there must be another way in.'

The Judoon started to move around the room, tapping the walls. The Doctor did the same the thing, listening carefully to the sound.

'These walls are solid,' reported the Judoon.

'But this one isn't,' replied the Doctor triumphantly and played a little drum roll on the wall with both hands to prove his point. 'This wall must have been put in after the lockers.'

The Judoon marched across to take a look for himself. 'In that case it is the weakest part of the structure,' he concluded. Without warning he pulled his arm back and punched forward. The metal surface of the wall crumpled, leaving a massive indentation. The Judoon punched again and again but, although the metal bent and twisted, it did not break.

The alien stopped to contemplate the damage he had inflicted so far. 'Nearly there,' he announced and then took a few steps away from the dented part of the wall, lowered his head and charged. His larger horn ripped into the weakened part of the wall and burst through. A second run widened the hole and then, with his gloved hands, the Judoon was able to peel the wall back like the lid of a tin of sardines to create a gap large enough for them all to pass through.

'That wall-bursting thing could become a nasty habit,' commented the Doctor as he climbed carefully through the jagged-edged hole.

The Judoon, carrying the moaning figure of Golightly, followed him.

'That could make me a crashing bore,' he said sternly and made the strange noise that the Doctor now knew to be laughter.

'Oi! Leave the appalling puns to me,' the Doctor said with a grin. 'I've got form. Right, *allons-y*. First priority: some medical attention for our friend here, and then…' He trailed off.

'What?' asked the Judoon, clearly still smarting about the way they had allowed their prize to be taken from them by Moret.

'Then we'd better get that case back,' said the Doctor with grim determination. 'Before anyone else gets hurt.'

Moret hurried through the wet and slippery streets, oblivious to the downpour that was rapidly soaking him to the skin. His heart was beating quickly in his chest, his breathing was slightly laboured. Although he was navigating through the city on autopilot, dodging traffic without really seeing it, inside he was more alert than he had been for years.

It was like being back in combat. For the first time in as long as he could remember, he felt properly alive. Adrenalin was running through his system, activating old senses and awakening long-buried memories.

He had enjoyed being a soldier. Life had been brutally simple: he was paid to fight and to kill and to follow orders. For twenty years he did just that, defending his homeworld against aliens of all descriptions.

And then, without warning, his political masters and their enemies had rediscovered the lost arts of diplomacy. A new spirit of tolerance and understanding began to spread through the region. Peace treaties and ceasefires and talk of reconciliation became the new status quo. Warfare itself became unfashionable and outdated.

For a man like Moret, this had been a bitter pill to swallow. He left his home planet vowing never to return. Eventually he had pitched up in New Memphis desperate for work. One of Uncle's men had spotted him on arrival and recognised his potential, and soon he was secretly working for Uncle's organisation while running spaceport security. But Uncle had treated him no better than the politicians had back home, so now he had a new boss – the Widow. At last he had found an employer who would show him some respect.

The rain continued to fall from the sky in torrents. Moret blinked raindrops out of his eyes and crossed another street, slipping between the slow-moving traffic. A bus passed him, its wheels hitting a puddle where a drain was blocked and sending a huge wave of dirty water into the air and over Moret.

Barely looking at the bus, Moret pulled out a weapon, pointed it behind him and shot out one of the vehicle's front tyres. It careered out of control and shot across an intersection. Horns blasted and there was the sound of multiple collisions, but Moret never looked back. He was focused on just one thing. Getting this precious package to the Widow and, more importantly, getting the gratitude he deserved.

Golightly was sitting up in a hospital bed, looking pale but at least alive.

'I can't believe Moret is crooked,' he was saying, shaking his head to emphasise his disbelief.

The Judoon Commander just snorted but the Doctor nodded sympathetically.

'Well, that's humans for you,' he said. 'Great actors. Infinite capacity for deception.'

'Which is why so many galactic criminals are human,' muttered the Judoon.

The Doctor shot him an annoyed look and continued. 'Ah, but they also have an infinite capacity to do the right thing. Like Nikki,' he added looking directly at the Judoon.

The Judoon Commander took his point.

'If this human is now safe,' he began, nodding at Golightly, 'then we should go after the suitcase.'

'Do you need details of where Moret lives?' offered Golightly, acutely aware that his injury had caused the

Doctor and the Judoon to postpone an immediate pursuit of the traitor.

The Doctor shook his head firmly. 'He's not going home,' he said with confidence. 'He'll be taking that suitcase directly to the Widow herself.'

'Then it's time for another visit to the Spa,' the Judoon suggested with a nod of agreement. '*Allons-y!*'

Moret reached his destination and was quickly ushered into a waiting area beyond the main Spa. Inside he was searched by the sweaty bodyguard, Taron. The overweight newcomer patted him down efficiently and gave him the all-clear. Moret regarded him with suspicious eyes.

Taron was new to the Widow's outfit and had not been around when she had recruited Moret from Uncle's employ. It had happened very suddenly and without warning. Moret had gone to visit Uncle, under cover of using the Casino. Uncle had arranged for him to be brought up to his private suite of offices above the gambling halls where he had berated him for his stupidity. Moret winced at the memory of the way Uncle had treated him. Uncle had reminded him that his value as an informant was his impeccable record and reputation; to be seen gambling was to put all that in danger. Moret – like the good soldier he was – had stood blank-faced and let the verbal abuse roll over him. He had heard far worse from his commanding officers in his fighting days, and words had little effect on him. Suddenly, however, Uncle's attitude had changed. It was so sudden, it was almost as if a switch had been flicked and a whole new personality activated. A door had opened and a pretty pale young woman had entered the room. Uncle, suddenly smiling and gentle, had introduced Moret to his daughter, Hope. The girl had smiled shyly and shaken his hand with a limp wrist and a grasp so weak that he could barely feel the contact. Uncle had told Hope that Moret was an old friend and had placed an arm round his shoulders. Uncle squeezed tight, his fingers painfully burying themselves in the ex-soldier's flesh. All the while, Uncle had maintained his air of genteel happiness – the very image of the perfect host. Finally Moret had managed to extricate himself, make credible excuses and get away. At the door, he'd given one last glance back into the room. Hope, the daughter, had been waving at him with a vacant or perhaps wistful expression on her face; behind her, Uncle had been standing with one hand raised in a gesture of goodbye while his eyes burned with contempt and anger. Moret had left the meeting determined to extract himself from Uncle's employ and, as luck would have it, that very evening he was contacted by the Widow.

That had been some months earlier, and Moret had been here a number of times for clandestine meetings with his new colleagues. At first, Moret had been a frequent sounding board for the Widow as she outlined plans and constructed strategy, but more recently Taron had usurped that role. That would have been enough on its own to engender antipathy towards Taron in Moret but there was more. Moret prided himself on having developed excellent instincts over the years. On the battlefield, it operated like a sixth sense, warning him of danger. In civilian life, it just reacted to people when he met them, giving him an intrinsic gut feeling about who he could and could not trust. When it came to Taron, Moret did not trust him as far as he could throw him. There was something about the man that set every warning bell in Moret's head ringing but what exactly it was he couldn't say. In public, the men tolerated each other but when together their eyes were rarely far from each other, ever vigilant.

Taron completed the body search and with a non-specific grunt indicated that Moret should enter the suite behind him. Picking up his precious cargo – the suitcase – Moret opened the door and went in.

Outside the Spa, the Judoon Commander found a place of concealment and settled down to wait. After a lot of discussion it had been agreed that it would be best, on this occasion, if the Doctor attempted to get inside the Widow's base of operations on his own. In fact, now that the Judoon Commander thought about it, although there had been an illusion of discussion, the Doctor had done most of the talking. Humans liked to talk, the Judoon Commander had noticed and, although the Doctor was not human, he clearly shared a lot of characteristics with the race and not just the obvious physical ones.

The Doctor was a strange case. The Judoon's experience of humans was relatively limited, but in most of his encounters with them the alien had found them to be essentially simple creatures. Not particularly trustworthy, or complicated, they tended to look after number one and talk a lot. In contrast, the Judoon found the Doctor utterly trustworthy and full of honour. Although he seemed uninterested in military matters, the Judoon was sure that there was some conflict in the Doctor's past. Beneath his energy and relentless enthusiasm for all and sundry, there was a sadness and a bitterness that just occasionally an observant viewer could spot.

Just now had been a typical example. The Doctor had all but waltzed off, grinning with anticipation at trying to get back inside the Widow's domain, armed with nothing but his sonic tool and a quick wit. The Judoon had urged caution and had reminded him of Nikki's situation, but that had only seemed to make him more manically cheerful. 'Don't get your horns in a knot,' the Doctor had said, grinning wildly. 'I'll be back before you know it.'

With that, the Doctor had disappeared into the Spa, leaving the Judoon to wait in the rain. That had been half an hour earlier. Since then, nothing of any significance had happened.

Suddenly, the Judoon Commander became aware of a presence behind him and felt the cold barrel of an energy weapon being pressed into the back of his neck.

'Turn around slowly,' hissed a voice in his ear.

Carefully, the Judoon Commander did as he had been asked.

FIFTEEN

When the Doctor left his Judoon companion, he crossed the street towards the Spa but did not enter the building. Instead, he walked past the notices offering facials and head massages, keeping his eyes directed at the pavement itself. In a side street, he saw what he had been looking for – a manhole cover. It took a little effort to lift the heavy metal cover – for a moment he considered going back to get the Judoon's assistance – but finally the heavy disc shifted in his hands and he was able to pull it clear. The shaft beneath was pitch black, but the sonic screwdriver provided enough light to reveal a metal ladder descending into the sewer system. The Doctor began to climb down, pulling the cover back. It dropped into place with a loud clang, shutting out the sounds and light from above.

Moving carefully on the ill-maintained and rusty ladder, the Doctor soon found himself at the bottom of the shaft in a wide cylindrical tunnel. His eyes had adjusted to the lack of light and he was able to make out some details of his surroundings. A central channel in the lowest part of the tunnel was a river of raw sewerage, which gave the environment a distinctive and quite unpleasant odour. To the Doctor's relief, there was a flat walkway built into the side of the tunnel, allowing access without the need to wade through the foul stream itself. The Doctor quickly took his bearings and headed in the direction of the Spa.

The Doctor was working on the theory that the underground systems of sewerage and transport would be connected at some point, and his hunch proved right. He soon reached a much bigger, horizontal tunnel where the floor was covered with metallic rails rather than a river of waste. The Doctor smiled to himself, remembering previous adventures in underground transport tunnels. Usually they had involved unspeakable creatures, but the only monsters on this world were distinctly human in nature. Creatures like Uncle and the Widow, who used their gang members like chess masters casually sacrificing pawns, were far more horrifying than any so-called monster that he'd met. The Judoon may have been prone to overkill, as he had witnessed many times, but they were honourable. At least they believed in justice, even if their justice was sometimes rather harsh and inflexible. Here on New Memphis, there seemed precious little justice. People like Nikki and her father were the exceptions rather than the rule. Again the thought of Nikki, held hostage by Uncle, spurred the Doctor on. He had to find a way into the Widow's lair and retrieve that suitcase.

The Doctor stopped and applied his exceptional sense of direction before choosing which way to go. A few moments later, he was delighted to find himself entering an area that was lit by powerful lights.

Suddenly, someone or something grabbed him from behind.

'Give me one good reason not to kill you right now,' hissed an angry but familiar voice in his ear.

The Doctor sighed. It was Moret, and he didn't seem pleased to see him.

The Judoon Commander regarded his assailant with cool eyes. Somehow, this large and flabby human had managed to creep up on a trained Judoon officer of the law and take his weapon from its holster without him noticing. How was that possible? The Widow's bodyguard took a step back and flipped the weapon over, holding it by the barrel.

'I am not your enemy,' Taron stated simply and reached out, offering the weapon back to the Judoon. The galactic law officer opened his gloved palm to take back the weapon, but hesitantly, still not entirely sure that he should trust this corpulent human. Without taking his eyes from the man's face, the Judoon took back his weapon and slipped it back into its rightful place on his hip.

'Who are you, then?' he asked finally, his voice a low rumble.

Taron smiled mysteriously.

'The Widow is a criminal,' the Judoon stated, 'and you work for her, therefore…'

'I must be a criminal too,' the man finished the statement for him. 'Not necessarily.'

'Then explain yourself,' demanded the Judoon.

Rather than give a direct answer, the bodyguard reached into his pocket and produced a small metallic device.

'Take this,' he instructed, passing him what the Judoon could now see was one of the local communicator devices, similar in design to the one that Nikki had.

'The girl is safe,' he added, almost as if he was able to read the Judoon's mind. 'She's at large at Uncle's Casino – you can use that to contact her to confirm my story.'

The Judoon just looked at the device, tiny in his massive gloved hands and then at the stranger again.

'Go on,' insisted the bodyguard. 'Try.'

The Doctor had not given Moret one good reason not to kill him.

He had given him multiple reasons, firing off one after another in a long speech that tried the ex-soldier's patience long before the Doctor ran out of breath. The tactic had worked, however, and Moret had dragged the Doctor away to meet with the Widow.

She was in the room where he had encountered her before, dressed in another figure-hugging dress. She lay on her chaise longue and took a long look at the Doctor and his captor.

'You've excelled, Moret. Two deliveries in one night!'

Moret bowed his head. 'I hope I haven't embarrassed Mr Taron,' he said, in an even tone. 'It is, after all, his job to protect you, isn't it?'

The Widow frowned. 'Where is Taron, I wonder?'

'Perhaps it's his tea break?' offered the Doctor. He took a step forward. 'Look, this has all been a terrible misunderstanding. Classic really, the old suitcase switcheroo at the airport sort of thing. If you can just let me have my case back...'

The Widow raised a hand. 'Can you just stop babbling for a moment?' she demanded.

'It's all he seems to do,' agreed Moret, balefully.

'Babble? Babble!' complained the Doctor. 'What kind of idiot do you think I am? It's just there's a lot to say.'

'Well, it can wait,' insisted the Widow firmly. 'First I want to let Uncle know that we've... acquired his case. Then we'll decide what to do with you. Until then, Moret, if he opens his mouth, shoot him.'

The Doctor looked across at Moret to see how seriously he was going to take this order and saw the gun ready in his hand. Quickly he ran a hand along his mouth in a zipping motion and gave the Widow the thumbs up. The woman sighed and got to her feet. Behind her, the Doctor saw a large screen which was clearly connected to some communications equipment. A technician was operating the controls.

'Open Channel D and get me Uncle,' the Widow ordered. She turned and smiled at the Doctor. 'I'm going to enjoy this.'

The Judoon found himself happier than he might have imagined possible when he heard the human girl's voice whispering from the tiny communications device.

'You are free, Nikki?' he asked.

'Yeah, but I'm still here at Uncle's. Taron said it was a good idea,' she told him.

The Judoon glanced over at the bodyguard, watching him with patient eyes. 'You trust this Taron?'

There was a pause and then Nikki answered. 'Yeah, I do. Not sure why. Call it instinct.'

The Judoon grunted, taking the information in. 'Then I shall trust him myself. The Doctor has gone to get the suitcase. We will return with it shortly.'

The conversation over, the Judoon flipped the communicator closed and placed it in one of the pockets of his uniform.

'Thank you,' he said to Taron, genuinely. He was surprised at how worried he had been about the human girl, and how much better he felt now that he knew that she was relatively safe.

'I need to get back to my post,' Taron told him quickly, 'but there's one more thing I need to give you.'

He passed over a small card with a computer chip set in it. The Judoon examined it curiously.

'Another locker key?' he asked.

'Not exactly. It's a security override for the Widow's base. Access all areas. You may need it.'

Taron began to move away. 'When we meet again, keep my secret,' he requested. The Judoon nodded, and the mysterious bodyguard hurried away through the rain.

The Doctor watched carefully as the two crime lords confronted each other across their communications screens. The Widow was bristling with the excitement of the moment, triumphant at getting one over on her enemy. For his part, Uncle was comparatively still, angry but contained.

'Your Invisible Assassin isn't going to be very effective without his equipment, is he, Uncle?' the Widow crowed, revealing the suitcase.

Uncle said nothing. His expression was fixed in neutral, but a rich mixture of emotions burned in his eyes.

'You're getting old, Uncle. You're past it! It's time for you to move on. If only you had a son to pass the family business on to.'

As she spoke, the Doctor noted the Widow's body language with interest. She was shaking with emotion, leaning forward into the camera transmitting her image, as if she wanted to be there in person, parading Uncle's failure right in front of his face.

'I have no son,' he retorted calmly, 'and I will not allow my daughter into this world of violence. But I do not need to. I am not going anywhere.'

Uncle made a stab at defiance, but to the Doctor's mind there was something ringing false about his statement. It felt somehow... rehearsed. Yes, that was it. Somehow it wasn't as spontaneous as it should have been in the circumstances. It was almost as if Uncle had been expecting this call. Was that possible? The Doctor leant forward, about to contribute to the conversation himself, but Moret raised the gun slightly and he fell back into his enforced silence.

'We'll see,' countered the Widow. 'When I have the

secrets of the Invisible Assassin, perhaps you will be his next victim. Goodbye, old man.'

She waved a hand to the technician to terminate the connection. The image of Uncle disappeared from the large screen, but in the last second that his face could be seen the Doctor saw what appeared to be a triumphant grin cross the man's face.

Something wasn't right here. If only he knew what it was.

From her vantage point above Uncle's office, Nikki had watched the conversation between the crime lord and the Widow with interest. From where she was watching, she had a good view of Uncle's body language and he seemed calm and in control throughout, despite the apparent setback.

Uncle was not watching the screen alone. The Walinski brothers were also there, and a fourth person, who had arrived just before the call came through. For a while the identity of this new arrival eluded Nikki. But when the conversation ended she spoke, and Nikki instantly recognised the voice. It was the police officer, Corilli, who had set them up earlier.

'I don't get it, Uncle,' said Corilli. 'Why are you grinning? The Widow's got your stuff.'

Uncle laughed out loud. 'That's why you make such a good policewoman, Corilli,' he said, patting the woman on the shoulder. 'You're so lacking in imagination.'

Corilli frowned, her brows scrunching together to create deep furrows across her forehead. 'You wanted her to have the suitcase?' she asked finally, squeezing the thought out of her head like the last toothpaste in the tube.

'Brilliant. Make the lady Commissioner of Police!' Uncle replied.

'But why?' Corilli was still struggling to make sense of the situation.

Suddenly the humour vanished from Uncle's demeanour. 'Why?' he echoed the corrupt policewoman. 'I'll tell you why. Because there is no Invisible Assassin. Not in the sense of a person anyway. The Invisible Assassin isn't a person at all; it's a thing. A virus. An artificial bio-agent that kills.'

The policewoman's jaw dropped open. 'You're going to release a deadly virus in the city? Are you mad?'

'Mad? I'm furious,' retorted Uncle. 'But not suicidal. The virus is very special. Short-lived in an oxygen-based atmosphere.'

Uncle sat back in his chair and put his hands behind his head.

'Brilliant or what?'

'So what happens? How does it work?' asked Corilli.

Uncle leaned forward over his desk, placing his hands down.

'Couldn't be simpler. She opens the case; she releases the virus. Thirty seconds later…' Uncle slammed his hand down on the desk, making everything on it jump. 'She's dead!'

The Judoon Commander was beginning to almost enjoy being in the rain. His uniform was mostly waterproof, and the rain hitting the exposed skin of his head was quite refreshing. The only negative was the occasional drip which managed to slip between the collar of his uniform and his neck, but the discomfort of this was not too great to bear. The raindrops running over the wrinkles of his face were quite invigorating. He glanced over at the Spa and wondered if, perhaps, there was something to be said for some appropriate skin care. Something throbbed in his leg and he realised that it was the communications device given to him by Taron. He extracted it and flipped it open. It was Nikki.

'Listen, Jude, this is important. The Widow mustn't open the suitcase,' she told him urgently. Quickly she passed on everything she had learned from eavesdropping on Uncle. The Judoon listened carefully and promised Nikki that he would do what he could.

With the need for speed overriding the need for caution, the Judoon Commander dashed across the street and straight into the Spa. Screaming patrons, some of whom had only just recovered from his visit earlier in the evening, hurried out of his way. Using the override key that Taron had given him, the Judoon Commander accessed the lift to the lower levels.

Inside the Widow's lair, the atmosphere was strangely tense. Taron the bodyguard had recently arrived and had clearly been put out to discover Moret there. The fact that the spaceport security officer had managed to capture the Doctor whilst Taron had been strangely absent from his post was an additional slur.

'Taron, you disappoint me,' the Widow said. 'You nearly missed my moment of triumph.'

'My apologies, Madame Yilonda,' he replied, bowing his head.

'Never mind.' The Widow started to reach for the suitcase. 'You are in time for the main event.'

She leant over the suitcase and reached for the clasps.

Suddenly a new figure burst into the room. The lumbering bulk of the Judoon Commander ran directly towards the Widow. Both Moret and Taron stepped forward into his path but he bulldozed straight through them, pushing them aside like rag dolls.

'Stop!' he roared, 'don't touch that, or you will die!'

DOCTOR WHO

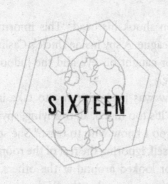

SIXTEEN

For a moment it was as if time had stood still. Moret and Taron got to their feet, and Moret immediately drew his weapon and pointed it at the Judoon Commander.

'Wait,' ordered the Widow. She looked down at the suitcase and then up at the alien.

'Explain yourself,' she demanded.

The Judoon took a moment to gather himself. 'It's a trap,' he said finally. 'The suitcase is a dummy. There is nothing in it except a virus. A deadly virus that will kill you!'

The Widow recoiled from the suitcase as if it were about to explode.

'So that's what they mean by an Invisible Assassin,' murmured the Doctor.

'How do I know this is not another trick? A double bluff. Has Uncle sent you here with this story, thinking me gullible?' wondered the Widow.

The Judoon shook his head. 'This information came from our colleague. A spy inside Uncle's Casino.'

The Doctor caught his eye and the Judoon nodded – Nikki was safe.

The Widow was pacing, trying to take in this latest information. 'It's too much, all this lying, spying, double-dealing, how do I know who to trust?' She seemed to be talking to herself, ignoring the rest of the room.

The Doctor looked around at the others. Moret was patiently waiting to see what the Widow would do next. He could see that the Judoon was readying himself for possible action but Taron was less patient. He took a step or two towards the suitcase and reached out to grab it. The Widow saw his movement and grabbed the gun out of a surprised Moret's hand. Before anyone could react or say anything, she shot her new bodyguard in the leg.

'Get back!' she screamed, with a distinct note of hysteria in her voice. She's losing it, thought the Doctor, she needs to be handled very carefully.

He raised his hands and took a step forward. 'It's OK,' he began but he got no further.

'OK? OK!' she bellowed. 'Nothing is OK. It's all gone wrong. Uncle's made me look a fool.'

Behind her, the Doctor could see Taron lying on the floor clutching his leg, his face a mask of agony. The Widow made an effort to pull herself together.

'Moret, there are secure storerooms down there.' She pointed off down a brick-lined tunnel. 'Lock these two in one of them.' She waved her purloined weapon at the Doctor and the injured Taron.

'What about the big guy?' asked the ex-security officer.

The Widow smiled for the first time since the Judoon Commander's arrival. 'I've got a little job for him.'

The Doctor was allowed to help Taron to his feet. The large man was not nearly as heavy as he looked. With the Doctor's support, he was able to walk down the tunnel to one of the storerooms. Moret pushed them roughly through the thick metal door and then secured it.

The Doctor listened to the heavy locks falling into position and then turned to look at Taron, who had found some boxes to sit on.

'Right then,' said the Doctor, with the air of a man whose patience had been severely tested. 'Why don't you explain exactly who you are, and why, when you're shot in the thigh, you don't appear to bleed?'

The Judoon Commander stood statue-still, waiting and watching as the Widow considered her next move. Between them lay the suitcase, its deadly virus still safely concealed within.

The woman finally stopped pacing and looked into the alien's deep-set eyes.

'Take it back to him,' she whispered. 'Tell him his Invisible Assassin has failed.'

She picked up the case and held it out for the Judoon Commander to take from her.

'And tell him that I expected more from him. An assassin is a coward's way of dealing with a problem. When word of this spreads – and I'll make sure it does – he'll be a complete joke. He's finished.'

Her smile grew wider but her eyes became even colder, hidden behind the cool blue of her oversized shades.

'Unless he cares to come to a compromise. I'm a reasonable woman. It's just possible that I could be persuaded to forget that this ever happened, for the right price.'

She stepped away and returned to her chaise longue. She settled herself down before continuing in a voice now rich with confidence.

'This is a big city and there's room for both of us. At least there will be if he withdraws from certain neighbourhoods and lets my people take over. Tell him I expect a first offer within twelve hours. And he'd better make it a good one!'

Nikki hadn't heard anything for an hour now. *What was happening?* She could only assume that things were not going well, but without contact from her friends she had no clue what to do next.

She had reacted instinctively to warn the Widow of the danger in the suitcase, but that act of humanity seemed to have backfired. The Doctor and the Judoon Commander had entered the Widow's base and just disappeared. Meanwhile, she was lurking around the access tunnels and ventilation shafts of the Casino like a rat in the wainscoting. It was like the business with her Dad. The best thing she could do was not to worry and keep busy. She decided that her best bet was to keep close tabs on Uncle and his people.

The crawlspace in the ceiling had become quite uncomfortable, so Nikki had managed to find somewhere to climb back down. Then, making sure that she wasn't seen by anyone, she explored the various rooms that made up this level of the building. There were guest rooms, mainly dormant, storerooms and various family spaces. There was also a room that reminded her of a meeting room or boardroom. It had seating for twelve at a large, highly polished table, surrounded on three sides by walls decorated with large screens. At the rear of the room were a number of sideboard-style cupboards, mostly filled with crockery.

Suddenly, Nikki heard the sound of approaching voices. As they came closer, she recognised the unmistakable tones of Uncle himself. Were they coming towards her? *Of course they are,* she told herself, *so make yourself scarce.* There was only one door to and from the room and no time to get on the table to access the crawlspace. She had little choice – it was either hide under the table itself or squeeze into the cupboards. Nikki took another quick glance at the cupboards and realised that they really weren't a viable option. She got on her hands and knees and crawled quickly under the table. It was oval and it bulged out quite widely in the middle, making an area that offered a degree of cover. As long as no one coming in had really long legs, she would be OK. *Hiding under the table,* she thought to herself with a grin. *What would Dad say to that?*

The Doctor was looking at the wound in Taron's leg. There was indeed no blood, just a rip in the skin and underneath that…

'Padding?' the Doctor frowned.

The man who had called himself Taron smiled and reached up to his neck. He tugged and pulled at the folds of skin around his neck and then began to pull his face off. It was a mask; a brilliant, lifelike prosthetic face. Underneath was a much thinner-faced man with the same lively eyes and grin as Taron but with radically different features.

'Detective Jupiter, I presume,' said the Doctor holding out a hand. 'I know your daughter.'

Nikki's father was continuing to remove his disguise. Underneath the padding and the Taron costume, he was wearing a lightweight suit. 'Excuse the smell,' he told the Doctor. 'It's pretty hot in that get-up.'

'I can imagine,' smiled the Doctor.

'Call me Conrad,' said the man, finally shaking the Doctor's hand.

'How long have you been undercover, Conrad?' asked the Doctor.

'Weeks. Tough case,' explained Conrad Jupiter. 'And it's been so full-on I've not been able to get word to Nikki. How is she?'

The Doctor pulled a face. 'Well, OK,' he answered. 'At least I think so. It's a bit complicated. She's kind of got a tough case of her own. And me and the Judoon are trying to help her.'

'And how's that going?' Nikki's father asked directly.

The Doctor wrapped a long arm around the back of his neck and scratched distractedly. 'Not too well,' he confessed. He frowned as another thought hit him.

'So tell me, what exactly were you undercover to find out?' he asked casually.

Conrad smiled. 'Something, anything, about the Widow, of course.'

'Any luck with that?'

'I've found out lots. About the Widow's operation, about the things that have been happening at Terminal 13, lots of stuff,' Conrad told the Doctor with some pride.

'But not who she really is or the real reason for her determination to bring down Uncle?' the Doctor pointed out, slightly deflating the detective. He shook his head sadly.

The Doctor turned away and began examining the walls for signs of weakness. 'She's Uncle's daughter,' he said casually, turning around to enjoy the look on the detective's face.

'Hope?!'

The Doctor nodded. 'Hope,' he repeated, and watched a bizarre set of expressions cross the man's face as he absorbed the information.

'But... what... she...' he spluttered on for a long moment, starting and stopping a dozen responses before sitting back down on his seat and shaking his head in amazement. 'A disguise?'

'Not quite as involved as the one you've been wearing – but a wig, change in make-up, different posture, body language. She's quite an actress,' explained the Doctor.

'But you saw through her,' Conrad was impressed.

'It's all in the hands,' the Doctor told him with a smile. 'Very hard to disguise hands.'

Conrad looked up at the Doctor, wide-eyed, shaking his head in amazement. 'Now you've told me, I can see it,' he agreed. 'At least I can see the *how*... but what about the *why*?'

'Dads and daughters,' muttered the Doctor by way of a reply. 'Difficult relationship. Can be, anyway...'

'So this crime war – all these deaths and beatings and gang warfare – it's all about a father and his daughter with relationship issues!'

The Doctor nodded. 'If only they could go on daytime TV and resolve things that way,' he joked. '"My Dad's A Crime Lord but he wants me to go to Finishing School", that sort of thing!'

Conrad stopped laughing as a fresh thought hit him.

'But the Widow's sent that case back to Uncle. Why would she do that? Unless...' he began.

'Unless she's tampered with it in some way,' continued the Doctor, following Conrad's train of thought.

'That virus could be released at any time. We need to get out of here and make sure Uncle doesn't open that case,' declared Conrad Jupiter determinedly.

The Doctor smiled approvingly. 'Right, then. First things first. How exactly do we get out of here?'

From her new hiding place, Nikki watched as various pairs of feet entered the room and took seats. Most seemed humanoid – wearing trousers and shoes, but one pair of feet, dressed in heavy boots, had a distinctly alien look. Nikki grinned to herself as she heard the now familiar tones of the Judoon Commander.

'With the compliments of the Widow,' announced the Judoon formally, putting something down on the table.

Nikki wondered what it could be.

'The Invisible Assassin,' the Judoon continued, answering Nikki's unspoken question. 'The Widow thinks it the weapon of a coward.'

Nikki could hear the sharp intake of breath that gave away Uncle's reaction to this statement.

The Judoon continued without pausing or allowing Uncle to get a word in. 'The Widow wanted me to pass on her terms for not letting the facts about your cowardly attack become public knowledge.'

Finally Uncle spoke. In a voice trembling with rage he demanded to know what she meant by terms.

'What does she want from me?' he demanded.

The Judoon explained. 'She wants a deal. "A slice of the action" – that is the phrase she used. A much bigger slice.'

Uncle grunted, as he processed the information. He was unable to take his eyes from the suitcase. Why was it back here? How could she have known? He refocused his attention on the alien's words. The Widow wanted a lot.

'And while we are talking of deals,' the Judoon Commander pressed on, 'what of the girl?'

Uncle's eyes remained focused on the suitcase. 'Girl? What girl?'

Charming, thought Nikki to herself.

'You held our friend hostage,' the alien reminded him.

'Never mind her, why didn't the Widow woman open the suitcase?' he demanded.

The alien looked back at him impassively, the narrow eyes set deep in his giant head regarding Uncle without blinking. There was a movement in the shoulders that might have been a shrug but might just as well have been the massive creature breathing.

'She should be dead,' insisted Uncle.

'The Widow is most certainly not dead,' the alien intoned, and made a sound which might have been a laugh. 'She said there had been a mistake. She'd been under the impression that this was a gift to her from you but now she realises her error she asked me to return it. Now – my friend. Where is she?'

Uncle nodded to the two heavies who lurked near to his desk. Both drew their weapons in preparation.

'She escaped,' he replied eventually. 'I don't know where she is now. Take him!'

The last was an order to his two underlings. They fired their weapons simultaneously, launching high-voltage electric shocks that hit the Judoon before he could begin to take any evasive action. Instantly, the alien lost consciousness, toppling over like a dislodged statue, landing face down on the table, and embedding his larger horn in the wood.

Beneath the table, the horn came within ten centimetres of extending the damage to Nikki's skull. She ducked down and started to crawl away from the point of impact, fearing that the table might collapse.

'Not so tough now, are you?' she heard Uncle muttering. 'Right, gentlemen. Back to business. Any reply from Golightly yet?'

Nikki heard no answer and could only assume that any reply had been a shake of the head judging by Uncle's response.

She heard him sigh heavily. 'What will it take before they close that place down? It should have closed the day it opened. All that lost luggage, all the delays, they should be on their knees.'

For a moment Uncle was silent, lost in thought and then, without warning, he slammed down his palms on the table. Nikki nearly jumped out of her skin.

'Activate the devices. If they won't close the place because of operational problems, perhaps a series of devastating terrorist attacks might change their minds.'

'What about the alien?' asked one of Uncle's men.

There was a long pause and then a throaty laugh as Uncle came up with an answer.

'Let's kill two birds with one stone,' she heard him say. 'We'll chain him up to the biggest bomb of the lot and splatter him across the whole terminal!'

Nikki's blood turned to ice in her veins as she listened to Uncle's next statement.

'One hundred separate explosions all over Terminal 13 – if that doesn't get their attention, nothing will. The Widow is nothing in this City, this is my territory, and after tonight everyone will remember that.'

SEVENTEEN

The Doctor had tapped and listened to the solid-sounding brick walls, examined the low ceiling with similar care and then turned to the floor. While Conrad watched, he knelt to examine the floor covering. It appeared to be old faded carpet. The Doctor scurried across to the wall and tried to insert his fingers between the edge of the carpet and the wall itself.

'So what did you find out about Terminal 13?' he asked unexpectedly.

Conrad was wrong-footed. 'Sorry?'

The Doctor gave the carpet a tug, but hadn't freed enough to get sufficient grip. 'You said you'd found out a lot about what's being going on at Terminal 13.'

Recovering, Conrad nodded. 'Yes, you could say that.'

'Who's behind it then – the Widow or Uncle?'

'What makes you think it has to be one of them?' asked

Conrad, his surprise at the question evident in his voice.

The Doctor grunted and pulled at the carpet again. This time it moved, ripping clear of ancient dried-out glue. 'Call it a hunch.'

'You don't believe it's the work of the direct-action branch of an environmental protection protest group, then?'

The Doctor looked up from his struggle with the carpet. 'Feel free to lend a hand,' he suggested.

'Sorry,' Conrad said, bending down to aid the Doctor in his task. Together, the men managed to pull the carpet further from the floor.

'It seemed clear to me that the missing luggage and the other problems were part of an organised pattern,' the Doctor explained, 'but I don't think that it's down to any kind of protest group. That sort of direct action tends to be more... spontaneous and sporadic. This has been relentless, cumulative...'

Slowly, the pair peeled the carpet back, rolling it up and revealing wooden floorboards below.

'You asked Uncle or the Widow; it was Uncle,' Conrad told the Doctor, who raised his eyebrows at the information.

'And the motive?' asked the Doctor. 'Why would Uncle want Terminal 13 shut down?'

'Uncle wouldn't,' smiled Conrad. 'But Salter does.'

'The man who built the place?'

Conrad was nodding again. 'He over-extended himself, apparently. Spent a fortune to build it, and now he can't afford to run it.'

'But surely when it's operational it's making some money. Why would having it closed be of any use to him?' asked the Doctor, genuinely confused.

He pulled his sonic screwdriver from an inside pocket and, after making a minute adjustment to the almost invisible controls on the device, he began using it to remove the nails from the floorboards.

Without needing to be told, Conrad began helping the Doctor lift the floorboards as the securing nails were removed.

'Economics, isn't it?' Conrad ventured. 'You're right. Common sense says keep the place open and keep some cash flow going, but it doesn't quite work like that. Basically, it's one of the oldest cons in the book… If Terminal 13 hadn't opened on time, Salter would have been hit with financial penalty payments that would have bankrupted him three times over. So it had to open when it did, come what may. Once that had happened, if it was then forced to close down, say for operational reasons or due to external factors like, well, sabotage or violent protests or something like that…'

Enough floorboards had been removed now to reveal some space underneath the floor – the bare bricks of the old tunnels the storerooms had been built into. The Doctor grinned and finished Conrad's sentence for him.

'Then there would be a massive insurance payout!' He dropped down into the hole.

'Exactly,' Conrad called after him. 'Like I said, it's the conman's classic – the insurance scam.'

'But on a really large scale,' commented the Doctor,

popping his head out of the hole. 'Are you coming?'

Conrad followed the Doctor down the hole and into the darkness beyond.

To Nikki's great relief, Uncle's musclemen had managed to remove the Judoon from the table without damaging it – or the Judoon – further. She'd watched from the far end of the underside of the table as four of Uncle's strongest had struggled to lift the unconscious alien onto a trolley and then wheeled him away. As soon as she was sure that the room was empty again, Nikki emerged from her hiding place and stretched gratefully. She seemed to have spent an awful lot of time recently in confined spaces and was looking forward to a shower and standing upright for a change.

First of all, though, she knew she had to do something about these bombs. From what she had gathered, Uncle had planted a hundred bombs in various locations around the new Terminal 13. Listening to Uncle discussing this with his men, she'd discovered that these devices had been placed months or maybe years ago during the construction of the new facility. They were like sleeper agents, ready to be woken when needed. And that's exactly what he had done just now: a signal had been sent, priming each device and initiating a countdown.

Nikki knew that the most important thing was to get some kind of warning out, but the more information she could give the authorities the better. Surely there must be some more data on these devices, maybe even some record of where they were located. And her current position, inside Uncle's headquarters, was the perfect place to find any such details.

Nikki moved out of the boardroom and started looking for somewhere with a computer terminal. Luck seemed to be on her side. Ever since her encounter with the mysterious Taron, things seemed to have been going right for her. She quickly secured the door of the room and activated the computer. Her dad had trained her in every aspect of IT from a very early age, claiming that information was the prime currency for a detective and that access to the wealth of information held on computers was a vital element in most investigations. Now was the time to put that training to the test.

The tunnel under the floorboards had been dark and unpleasant, but that had only been the beginning. The Doctor had soon found an access shaft leading to further tunnels, and together the detective and the Time Lord slowly descended further into the real underworld of New Memphis.

The lower they travelled, the more primitive the tunnels became, not to mention smaller and wetter. The only light came from the Doctor's multifunctional tool, the sonic screwdriver. Its pale blue glow managed to infect the darkness and allowed Conrad to make out his immediate surroundings but not, thankfully, the precise shapes of the small creatures that skittered and squealed around their feet as they moved through the tunnel.

To pass the time, the Doctor had been telling Conrad a little of their adventures thus far. Conrad was pleased that

Nikki had fallen in with such good company, although he confessed to having had his doubts about the rhino-headed alien.

'I know what you mean,' agreed the Doctor. 'I think I might have been a bit quick myself. Not like me to judge on appearances, don't like to do that as a rule. But you see those Judoon, marching about in those suits, and you just can't help yourself.'

'The one you've been working with seems OK, though, doesn't he?' Conrad suggested.

The Doctor grunted. 'Yeah, I really got him wrong. He's a bit of a joker on the quiet you know.'

'Really?' Conrad couldn't quite believe that.

'Yeah,' continued the Doctor, 'I reckon he should give up the galactic law enforcing and try a bit of stand-up. Ah, here we are.'

The Doctor held the sonic screwdriver high in the air, its blue light revealing a rusty metal ladder which disappeared upwards into a tall shaft.

'Bit of a downdraft,' mused the Doctor. 'Reckon that's the way out then. Who's going first?'

Nikki didn't know whether to laugh or cry. On the one hand, she'd succeeded beyond her wildest dreams – she had a full list of the locations for the bombs. But she also had details of the time fuses on each one.

The devices had staggered detonation times and, if the information she had was correct, the first of those bombs would explode just three hours after the priming signal. How long was it since she had been in the boardroom?

How long before that first explosion would tear through the terminal building?

Nikki looked at her communicator. Who to call? Half the police force were in the pocket of Uncle or the Widow or both. What about the authorities at the spaceport? But with the defection of General Moret, the security department would be in a mess. If only the Judoon Commander were with her – at least he'd be able to call down his legions.

That was it. The Judoon! Their ships were in orbit. They had teleport capability. And they had the manpower. All she had to do was make contact. She knew that there was no way her handheld communicator was up to the task. She'd need something a little more powerful than that to make her call. Would Uncle have something suitable? Could her incredible streak of luck hold out?

Nikki set off to look and, to her delight, it seemed that Uncle did indeed have just such a facility in this very building. But that was as far as her luck held. The communications room was permanently manned.

Currently there was a young man on duty, sitting at the main console, flicking through various channels including, Nikki noted with interest, police surveillance cameras and the security system at the spaceport. She was sure she could use this system to make contact with the Judoon ship, but she had to do something about the young man first. *Come on, girl*, she told herself. *He's a man. You know how stupid they are.*

She knocked at the door and composed herself into a vision of innocent confusion. Pitching her voice higher, she asked innocently, 'Excuse me, can you like help me or something?' The man swivelled in his seat to face her. He was younger than she had first thought.

She smiled sweetly at him and opened her eyes wider. 'Oh, I'm sorry, I can see you're busy…' Nikki turned to walk away, hoping she hadn't overplayed it.

'No wait,' said the young man.

She turned back quickly and took a step into the room.

'What are you doing here?' he demanded.

'I'm looking for the gaming hall. I went to the ladies and got lost… I think I got in the wrong lift,' she explained, maintaining her role perfectly.

'You really did,' the man replied, and to her relief he gave her a smile. 'What's a nice girl like you doing in a casino anyway?'

He got to his feet and started to cross the room towards her. Nikki gulped. She hadn't prepared this role in depth. She thought fast.

'I'm here with some girls from the office. It's Bali's hen do. I've never been anywhere like it. Isn't it exciting?'

She allowed the guy to put a hand on her elbow and lead her back into the corridor.

'I guess first time it is. After that it's a bit dull, if you ask me,' confessed the young man. He took her towards the lifts. 'I'll get you back to your friends, don't worry.' He jabbed a finger at the control to call the lift.

'Oh, but I don't really like lifts,' Nikki squealed, shivering as if in fear. 'Can I take the stairs?'

The man sighed, and again Nikki worried that she might be overegging the pudding, but he just crossed the hall and opened a door.

'Stairwell's down here,' he said with just a hint of impatience.

Nikki hurried across the hall and screamed, pointing into the stairwell. 'What's that? Is it a rat?'

The man leant forward to look in the direction she was pointing and she karate-chopped him on the back of the neck. The unfortunate technician went down like a sack of bricks. Nikki ran back to the communications room. As long as no one else was using the stairs – and who did these days – she should have enough time to make her call.

She shut the door behind her and, checking with her communicator where the Judoon Commander had stored the Judoon contact details earlier, she started to enter the frequency into the console.

The Judoon Commander stirred and began to open his eyes. It had been a long time since an enemy had rendered him unconscious. In fact, now that he thought about it, the last time he had been forced into unconsciousness had been in an undisciplined ruck during Basic Training, and that had been due to a pair of senior recruits double-teaming to take him down from behind.

He opened his eyes just a little at first in case he was being watched, but it was immediately clear that he was alone. Wherever he was, it was quite dark and cool.

He opened his eyes further and tried to move his head but discovered that he was chained tightly to a metal fixture. Near him, he could see a pack of explosives attached to an electronic timer. A small digital display showed a countdown. 1:31. Did he have ninety minutes or ninety seconds? He tried to pull at the chain but without any success.

The chain was made of thick metal links and was wrapped around his limbs and neck multiple times. His opportunity for movement was negligible. If he had been conscious whilst being chained he might have been able to make it harder for his captors to tie him so tightly, but instead he was as trussed up as it was possible to be. There was no way he was going to get out of here without assistance.

All he could do was hope that the Doctor and Nikki would find him – and soon. He looked over at the readout. 1:30. Ninety minutes then.

Ninety minutes to live.

Talking to the Judoon fleet proved to be harder than Nikki had originally imagined.

'Ro, Mi, Do, Ro-Ma,' the Judoon had barked at her, as soon as a visual connection was established. Having spent some time with the Judoon Commander, Nikki could see how different the individual Judoon were. This one looked much younger than 'her' one, with smaller tusks and less wrinkly skin. He also seemed a little bit dimmer.

'Er, hello. Do you speak Standard?'

The Judoon on her screen frowned and then fiddled with something off screen. She heard her voice played back and then, to her relief, the Judoon began to make sounds she could recognise as words.

'This is an official Judoon command channel. Unauthorised communication is not allowed. Immediate termination will ensue,' barked the Judoon, quoting chapter and verse from his training manual.

'No, wait a mo,' shouted Nikki urgently. 'I have a message from your Commander.'

'Commander?'

'Commander Rok Ma,' she clarified.

There was a long moment while the communications officer considered this new information.

'Wait,' he said eventually, and the screen went blank.

'No, don't put me on hold,' wailed Nikki but it was too late, the screen had gone blank. Nikki tapped her fingers nervously and waited. *At least they're not playing me some annoying music,* she thought.

Finally, after what seemed like hours but was probably just a couple of minutes, the screen flickered back into life. Another Judoon had now joined the first. This one proved to be a little bit more imaginative and intelligent that the first.

'Why has Commander Rok Ma asked a local to contact us? Where is he?' demanded the new arrival.

'It's a long story,' sighed Nikki.

She patiently explained the entire situation. To her relief the Judoon seemed to get the message, finally.

'Upload your data concerning the location of these explosive devices,' the more senior alien instructed her. 'Judoon bomb-disposal teams will be deployed by teleport.'

Relieved that some action to deal with the threat was now being taken, Nikki's attention turned to her friends. The Judoon's question had been a sound one. Where exactly had the Judoon Commander been taken? And what had happened to the Doctor? If only her dad was with her. Nikki felt more alone than she had felt for years.

She glanced up at the various TV screens and her heart jumped. There on one of the screens, approaching the exterior of the Casino, were two unmistakable figures. Damp, dirty but unbowed it was the Doctor and...

'Dad!'

EIGHTEEN

The Doctor smiled as Nikki hugged her father. The final part of their journey had been the easiest as locked Casino doors had mysteriously opened for them and lifts seemed to have been sent to collect them. The Doctor quickly figured out that Nikki had access to the control systems and was aiding them, but said nothing to Conrad. So when the lift doors had opened on the floor above the Casino and Nikki had been there to meet them, there was a wonderful parade of emotion across the detective's face from surprise to disbelief and then to complete delight.

It was Nikki who broke the embrace first, however. Quickly she filled them in on the situation with the bombs and the solution that she had found.

'You called down the Judoon?' the Doctor asked in awe. 'And they're coming?'

'I managed to persuade them. I pointed out that their

Commander was in danger; that seemed to do the trick,' she explained.

'Got to be careful with Judoon,' muttered the Doctor. 'They'll try and arrest the whole planet if anything happens to him.'

The Doctor questioned Nikki about the bombs – when she discovered the information about their locations, had there been any indication of a deactivation control?

'If they could be primed by a single signal, there's a chance that they can be turned off the same way,' he explained.

'There was something, but it was password protected,' said Nikki.

'Something else for me to discuss with Uncle,' muttered the Doctor, 'and another reason to keep him alive. He doesn't seem like the kind of man who would write a password down anywhere.'

'What about the Judoon Commander?' asked Nikki. She explained about his capture and what Uncle had decided to do with him. 'The bombs are on offset timers. With any luck, the Judoon will deal with most, but they might not get to them all in time. If we can't get the password, Rok Ma might still be killed.'

'Let's go rescue him, then,' suggested Conrad, leading Nikki towards the lifts. 'It's the least we can do after all he's done for us.'

Jase Golightly, bandaged and on crutches, watched the alien policemen swarming like ants all over his Terminal 13, for the second time in as many days. On this occasion, however, he was quite pleased to have them there. Delighted, in fact. One by one, the Judoon were finding and dealing with the explosive devices.

It was taking a long time, though. Each location from the information downloaded by Nikki was an approximation, and each device had been well hidden, sometimes built into the actual structure of the building. Uncle's plans had been made a long time ago, and his people had been able to infiltrate the army of builders and construction workers who had made Terminal 13. The seeds of the new facility's destruction had been incorporated into its very structure. Getting at those devices now required a certain amount of effort. Watching one team of Judoon dismantling a wall, Golightly wondered for a moment if the bomb itself wouldn't do less damage, but then one of the aliens had accidentally triggered the detonator. The explosion was instant and devastating. When the dust settled, Golightly saw that the damage it had caused was extensive. All three aliens working on that site had been killed instantly. And this had been just one bomb. One of a hundred. Golightly swallowed hard, realising just how much danger the entire terminal was in. Whatever the cost, the Judoon had to find and disarm the bombs.

So far, the Judoon had located forty-seven of the hundred devices; one had just exploded, thirty-two had been disarmed or rendered inactive, thirteen had tamper-prevention circuitry which was causing the Judoon bomb-disposal experts some problems, and the final one had just begun to accelerate its timer when it had been exposed to the air. Judoon were continuing to work on the device while some of their colleagues were evacuating the immediate area. From his vantage point, looking out over the terminal from his office, Golightly watched in horror as a section of wall disappeared in an orange ball of flame.

The Doctor approached Uncle's office but, before he could enter, two familiar dark-suited, white-haired figures appeared in the corridor and barred his way.

'The brothers Walinski, hello,' said the Doctor. 'Sorry but I don't have time for any meaningless violence right now.'

The brothers looked at each other then back to the Doctor and shrugged. They weren't interested in what he had time for. He took another step forward and they tensed, ready for action.

'Actually,' continued the Doctor in the same casual tone, 'I never have any time for meaningless violence.'

He took another deliberate step forwards and the brothers, moving in unison like synchronised divers, both struck at the Doctor's neck. The twin blow should have killed their opponent on impact, but there was no impact. Instead, somehow, the stick-thin interloper had grabbed each of their arms and squeezed. Suddenly both brothers were on their knees as paralysing pain shot up their arms and into the rest of their bodies. The Doctor released his grip on their wrists and stepped past the two brothers, who knelt frozen in place like statues. Slowly, but still in perfect synchronisation, the brothers toppled over onto the floor, out cold.

The Doctor liked to make a big entrance whenever

possible, so he flung open the doors to Uncle's office.

'Right, sunshine,' he announced, 'time to get serious.'

Uncle was sitting at his desk, his chair turned around so he could look at the bank of monitors to the side of the room. He showed no sign of having heard the Doctor at all.

'Oi! I'm talking to you!' The Doctor was getting a little angry now. Still the crime lord failed to react. A terrible thought occurred to the Doctor. He moved further into the room. The suitcase which had caused so much trouble was lying on the floor close to the desk. As the Doctor came closer, he could see that it was open. The virus had been released.

The Doctor ran the rest of the way across the room and spun Uncle's chair round. The man was ashen and almost completely paralysed, but there was still life in him. His chest heaved with the effort of breathing and his eyes met the Doctor's, full of questions. But the Doctor had questions of his own.

'Why open the case? Are you crazy?' he demanded.

Uncle managed to shake his head a little.

'It shouldn't affect me. It's a... targeted virus.'

'Targeted?'

'On... specific DNA...'

The Doctor bowed his head, finally understanding.

'You got a sample of the Widow's DNA and had the virus constructed to attack just that DNA?' he whispered.

Uncle nodded.

'Oh I'm sorry. I'm so sorry,' muttered the Doctor with genuine emotion.

The dying man struggled to speak.

'I don't underst…' he gasped.

'Understand?' completed the Doctor. 'No, I can see that. You're a brute and a bully. You create discord and fear and encourage the worst aspects of humanity. And you don't understand why people keep thwarting your will, and trying to close down your operations. You know why that is? Because most people are decent and honest. Most people want to play by the rules. Most people want to treat other people fairly.'

'Like my Hope…' Uncle suggested, his words no more than a faint whisper now.

The Doctor ran a hand through his hair, taken aback by the depth of the man's ignorance.

'Hope? Your daughter, the teacher in the pretty dresses, with the perfect manners? She's the reason you're in this state!'

The Doctor could see that Uncle had no idea what he was saying.

'You commissioned an invisible assassin, a DNA-coded virus to take out the Widow, Madame Yilonda? But when it came back to you and she was still alive, you had to have a look yourself, didn't you? See if something had gone wrong. But it hadn't. The system was still intact until you went and opened the box. And then the virus attacked you.' The Doctor paused. 'Why do you think it did that?'

The Doctor saw the poor man's eyes widen as the implication sank in.

'Yes, because you share the same DNA as the Widow. Your enemy Yilonda is Hope – your daughter.'

The Doctor sat on the desk and let this sink in. 'Tell me the password to stop the explosions. Make the last thing you do a good thing.' He knelt to look the dying man in the eye. 'Please. Haven't enough people died?'

The crime lord looked as if he was about to reply, but no sound emerged. Uncle was dead. And his secret had died with him.

Nikki and her father reached Terminal 13 to find a scene of utter chaos. Judoon were everywhere, searching out the various bombs and trying to disarm them. The emergency services were dealing with the aftermath of the two devices that had gone off, trying to contain fires and avoid collapsing masonry.

The two detectives located Golightly and cross-referenced his data on which devices had been located with Nikki's original list. They quickly established that the Judoon Commander himself had not yet been found.

'If Uncle's men brought him here tonight,' reasoned Conrad, 'then it must be an area of the terminal that is easy to access.'

'It's a secure site,' complained Golighty indignantly. 'No one can just stroll in here.'

'But that's the point,' Nikki responded. 'They must have.' She had an idea. 'Can you pull up the full schematics for the terminal – the original plans?'

Golightly hesitated. 'They are not meant to be public documents.'

'We're trying to save lives not steal secrets,' Nikki told him firmly.

Golightly turned away from the viewing window and crossed the room to his computer terminal. Quickly, he called up the files Nikki had requested. She then overlaid the data on the location of the explosive devices. Conrad and Nikki looked at the combined graphic closely.

'There,' said Conrad finally, jabbing at the screen with a stubby finger.

He was pointing at an access tunnel, at the lowest basement level which connected to the adjacent terminals. Golightly leaned over their shoulders to look.

'Emergency cross-terminal access tunnel,' he explained. 'Usually deadlock sealed.'

Conrad looked at him. 'How much do you want to bet that the locks are off right now?'

The Doctor stared at the viewscreen and waited. It was a long shot but it was the only option he had. Unless someone else knew the secret. Someone really close to Uncle.

He had made the call and asked to speak to the Widow. The receptionist at the Spa had made a big play of not knowing what he was talking about, but the Doctor had ignored the pretence. 'Just get this message to her. I need to talk to her urgently. Tell her it's about Hope,' he had said clearly.

The receptionist had put him on hold and then, a moment or two later had come back and told him to stand by. That had been two minutes ago. Was the Widow going to take his call or not?

Finally the screen flickered back into life, and he was

looking at the face of the Widow – Madame Yilonda.

'You can take off the disguise,' the Doctor said simply. 'I know who you are, Hope.'

For a moment nothing happened and the Doctor wondered if his audio signal was not getting through, but then the woman on the screen removed her oversized tinted glasses and reached up to take the dark-haired wig off her head. Underneath, her natural blonde hair was tightly coiled but the transformation was still striking. Where a moment ago he had been looking at the face of Madame Yilonda, he was now seeing the gentle features of Uncle's daughter, Hope. When she spoke it was with the much lighter voice of Hope.

'You're a perceptive man, Doctor,' she told him. 'Unlike my foolish father.'

'Your *late* foolish father,' the Doctor said simply. 'I'm sorry.'

He expected delight, but in fact the news seemed to shake Hope badly.

'Dead?' she asked, obviously in shock.

'That's what you wanted, isn't it?'

'I- I don't know,' she stammered. 'I just wanted him to care.'

To the Doctor's surprise, she began to cry and, as the tears fell, words tumbled from her lips.

'He shut me out. From when I was tiny. Maybe he wanted a son, I don't know. But he never wanted me to know anything about him or his work. It was like I didn't know him…'

'I'm so sorry,' murmured the Doctor.

'I thought maybe when I turned eighteen things would be different. That he'd let me in. But he didn't. So I created the Widow. As a way to get back at him…'

She wiped a hand across her face, drying the tears, and as she did the harder edge of the Widow crept back into her voice.

'I wanted to be part of his life, but he wouldn't have it. So I had to find a way to force the issue. I wanted to take his empire bit by bit until he had nothing. And then I was going to tell him the truth.'

Hope – or was it Yilonda – pulled herself together. 'Is that why you called? To tell me he's dead?'

The Doctor shook his head. 'I need your help,' he replied, and explained about the situation with the bombs and the password.

'Your secret need not come out. The Widow can just disappear. As Hope you can take over Uncle's legitimate businesses and start a new life. Just help me work out the password.'

Golightly had not taken Conrad's bet – which was just as well for him as the massive circular metal doors to the emergency tunnel were completely unlocked. Half a kilometre along the cold and dark tunnel they found the Judoon Commander. The readout on the explosive device was down to 9:45 – less than ten minutes.

'Don't worry,' Nikki told the Judoon Commander. 'We'll get you out of there.'

'There's no time,' he insisted. 'Get away from here before it's too late.'

Conrad was following the chain, looking for whatever it was that was securing it. 'Got it,' he exclaimed. The chain was held by a single massive padlock.

Golightly took one look at it and cheered. 'It's one of ours. They must have used spaceport materials.'

Conrad looked at him. 'You have a key?'

Golightly nodded and sent a Judoon trooper to his office to fetch the necessary key.

Nikki looked at the countdown. Eight minutes.

Hope was trying, but without success.

'He never had a pet name for me when I was little,' she told the Doctor, a little sadly. 'I never saw him much.'

'What about your first pet? A favourite family holiday destination. Your first cuddly toy?' suggested the Doctor.

Hope shook her head. 'We never had any of those.'

The Doctor snapped his fingers. 'Your mother! What was her name?'

Hope stared at the Doctor, the tears rolling down her face again. 'I don't know... I never knew her. She died giving birth to me. And that's all I know.'

'Thank you,' said the Doctor. 'At least you tried.'

'But what happens now? To me? The virus is loose in the atmosphere. Will it kill me too?'

The Doctor looked grim. 'I really don't know. Right now, if I were you, I'd leave the planet at the first opportunity and let things cool down before you come back.'

The Judoon trooper returned with the key, and within moments his Commander was free. The timer on the bomb now read 2:15. The Judoon Commander looked around at their position.

'If this explodes, the damage will be extensive,' he muttered.

'I think I can disconnect the detonator,' said Conrad, examining the device.

'Dad – no, it's too late!' Nikki screamed.

Conrad looked at the Judoon Commander. 'Get her to safety please.'

The Judoon Commander nodded and picked up Nikki in one arm. He barked something at the Judoon trooper in his own language, and the trooper grabbed Golightly in a similar fashion. The two Judoon then set off down the tunnel at full speed, putting as much distance as they could between themselves and the explosive device.

'Dad!' screamed Nikki desperately, pummelling the Judoon Commander's back with her fists, but Conrad had already turned back to the task at hand. The Judoon surged onwards back towards the massive door at the end of the tunnel.

The last thing she saw as they disappeared around the curve of the tunnel was her father hunched directly over the device and the glowing red numerals on the timer: 1:58… 1:57… 1:56…

The Doctor returned to Uncle's corpse and gently closed the dead man's eyes.

'Excuse me,' he said unnecessarily, and began to search through Uncle's pockets. There was nothing in them – no wallets, no family photos, nothing. The Doctor slipped his glasses on and looked around the desk. Nothing personal here either. Surely he would have something. Humans always kept mementos, keepsakes, rings…

Of course, thought the Doctor, rings. Throughout the known universe the ring was a symbol of unity between life mates. He checked Uncle's hands. There was a ring – a plain band on his wedding finger.

He slipped the ring from the dead man's hand. It took a bit of effort – the ring had clearly not been removed often. Inside there was an inscription: a date and two names. Vikta and Malinda. Bingo.

The Doctor hurried across to the computer console.

The Judoon burst out of the tunnel back into the basement level of Terminal 13 and put down their human cargo. Immediately, Nikki made to run back into the tunnel, but the Judoon Commander was too quick for her and held her back.

'No,' he said with surprising gentleness. 'I promised your father I would keep you safe.'

The Doctor typed the word 'Malinda' in and pressed enter. He held his breath and then the screen reset, giving him access to the override. Quickly, he sent the signal to cancel the remaining explosions.

The Judoon Commander was shaken by a massive explosion from within the tunnel.

'No!' screamed Nikki. But it was too late.

NINETEEN

The Doctor had done it. The cancellation signal deactivated all of the remaining devices and then, at a less frantic rate, the Judoon were able to render each and every one of them safe. For a while, all was chaos as emergency services dealt with the aftermath of the crisis. It took some time before the Doctor could be reunited with his friends at the spaceport. When he finally found them, Nikki was in a state of shock and the Judoon Commander was doing his best to comfort her.

'Conrad?' asked the Doctor when he joined them. Leaving Nikki sipping from a hot drink, the Judoon Commander shook his head gently and joined the Doctor.

'He wanted to try and disarm the bomb in the tunnel,' he explained.

The Doctor looked appalled. 'Don't tell me I was too late?'

The Judoon shrugged his massive shoulders. 'There was an explosion. The tunnel collapsed. Rescue teams are trying to get in there now.'

The Doctor glanced over at Nikki. 'How is she?'

The Judoon shrugged again.

Suddenly there was a commotion from the direction of the tunnel. A couple of firemen wearing brightly coloured uniforms appeared, dragging an anti-gravity stretcher behind them.

Nikki jumped to her feet, seeing a human form on the stretcher. 'Dad?'

One of the firemen glanced up at her. 'Your father's a lucky man. He'll need to spend some time in hospital, but he should make it.'

'He survived the bomb?' asked the Judoon.

'The bomb never went off,' the fireman explained. 'He must have managed to separate the detonator from the main explosives and hurl it away. The detonator went off and brought the tunnel down but the main explosives never fired.'

Nikki couldn't help herself and began to cry tears of joy.

'We'd better get him to the ER,' said the fireman.

Nikki turned and flung her arms around the Judoon, who looked startled. 'We did it,' she declared, giving the alien a huge hug. 'We really did it.'

Over her head, the Judoon looked at the Doctor who couldn't help but laugh at the sight before him.

'Just a few loose ends to sort out now,' declared the Doctor. 'Like Mr Salter.'

'That's all in hand,' said a new voice. The Doctor turned and saw that they had been joined by Detective Dantin and, still on his crutches, Jase Golightly.

'In fact, we're just off to pick up Salter now,' Dantin told them. 'Would you care to join us?'

The Doctor glanced at his friends.

'I think I'd prefer to go to the hospital,' said Nikki.

'But I would like to see this Salter arrested,' the Judoon rumbled, with enthusiasm.

'Me too,' said the Doctor.

Salter was not hard to find. He lived in a massive tower block known, modestly, as Salter Towers, which dominated the downtown skyline. On the ground floor it housed an upmarket mall where some of the most exclusive designer labels in the sector could be found. Above that was a five-star hotel, and above that were Salter's own private apartments. The building was decorated with lots of strange and outlandish design features. Statues of mythical creatures were attached to the roof; massive overhanging balconies clung to the sides of the building like limpets, and the walls themselves curved upwards, making the tower block wider at the top than at its base. It was the most original-looking building in all of New Memphis.

Armed police in flak jackets and lightweight body armour swarmed around the base of the tower like ants. The Doctor and the Judoon Commander were impressed at the military-style operation that Dantin had put together so quickly. Time was of the essence. With the collapse of the bombing campaign, Salter had to be aware that his role in the plan was about to become public knowledge. Dantin was determined, however, that Salter would not escape justice. He knew they had to move fast. 'Justice must be swift,' he had said, with a nod of acknowledgement in the direction of the Judoon Commander.

Dantin gave the order to go in. The officers entered the building in waves, securing and then searching each area, then each floor, before moving on.

'Almost like Judoon,' muttered the Judoon Commander as he and the Doctor looked on from Dantin's command position.

'But is that a good thing?' asked the Doctor in a hushed whisper.

'Not necessarily,' the alien whispered back. The Doctor grinned – clearly lessons had been learned.

Slowly the reports came back in from the search parties. Floor by floor they were giving an all-clear – no sign of Salter. Soon the police had moved through the mall levels and the hotel above and were ready to move on to the private apartments.

'That's where we'll find him,' Dantin told his guests confidently.

The Doctor and the Judoon exchanged looks, not sharing Dantin's confidence.

They were not surprised twenty minutes later when the searchers reported a total lack of success. They had covered all the emergency stairwells and shut down each elevator; they were certain that Salter had not had the opportunity to escape, but nevertheless they had been unable to find the man. Dantin was both furious and bemused.

'We have him on a security camera entering a lift two hours ago,' he explained, 'and the lift went up. He has to be in that apartment.'

The Doctor and the Judoon Commander followed Dantin into the building to see for themselves.

'Which elevator did he go into?' asked the Doctor.

Dantin showed him. 'It's a private lift to the top five floors which are exclusively Salter's private areas; the lift doesn't stop on any other floors,' he explained.

Dantin was called away by one of his men to look at the latest enhancement of the grainy security video, leaving the Doctor and the Judoon at the private lift. The alien jabbed a thick gloved finger at the call button and the indicator above the doors lit up to show that a lift was coming down from above.

'Salter entered the lift and went up,' the Judoon stated, 'and it doesn't seem to have come down again, so logically the man must still be up there.'

'And yet the police couldn't find him.'

The lift arrived with a ping, and the doors slid open silently. The Doctor instantly stepped inside and the Judoon followed him. He watched with interest as the Doctor produced his slim sonic device from his jacket pocket.

'Did you notice anything about this building when we were outside?' asked the Doctor suddenly.

The Judoon frowned. 'Only that it was bigger than it needed to be.'

'Yeah, you're right,' the Doctor nodded and adjusted the settings on his sonic device. 'It's all a bit over the top, isn't it. Demanding to be looked at. It draws your eyes to certain parts of the design. Like a magician directing your gaze to where he wants you to look.'

'You think it's some kind of trick?'

The Doctor zapped the lift controls with a blast of sonic energy. The lift responded by closing the doors. A moment later, it started to rise with an almost imperceptible motion. The numbers on the readout began to rise; 1, 2, 3...

'Salter's penthouse is meant to have five floors,' the Doctor told the Judoon, 'but if you actually look at the building from the outside, the windows are the wrong size. There's a hidden floor!'

The readout reached 5 and the lift stopped. The Doctor frowned, adjusted the settings on his sonic tool again and aimed it at the controls. The lift began to move again. 'That's more like it,' muttered the Doctor, pocketing his device. 'Mr Salter really wants to keep his secrets...'

A few seconds later, the lift stopped and the doors opened.

'But secrets are meant to be discovered,' said the Doctor with a smile.

He stepped forward and found himself in a corridor. The Judoon hurried out after him.

'I'll go left,' suggested the Doctor, 'you go that way. But first...' The Doctor turned back to look at the lift and fired another zap of compressed sound at it from his pencil-like tool. 'I'll just lock this in case he manages to slip past us.'

The Judoon nodded and set off in the direction the Doctor had indicated. He gripped his weapon in his hand. Salter had been responsible for the deaths of a number of

Judoon officers, and the Commander was determined that, for Salter, justice would be both swift and deadly.

The Doctor moved slowly along the corridor, which gave access to a number of rooms. From somewhere nearby, he could hear the sound of talking. Had the Judoon found their man first?

The Doctor increased his pace and soon reached the source of the noises. It was a large room, mostly in darkness. A massive viewscreen was displaying a newsfeed about the success of the police in thwarting the terrorist action at Terminal 13.

Sitting in front of the screen with a drink in his hand was Salter.

'You must be disappointed,' said the Doctor with savage sarcasm. 'No one seems to be giving you the credit.'

If the Doctor had been hoping to surprise Salter, he was disappointed. The man calmly turned his wheelchair around, as if he had been expecting the Doctor.

'It's not *the* credit I need,' Salter replied. 'It's just credit.'

The Doctor sighed. 'All this death and destruction – and it's all about something as trivial as money?'

'It's always about money, Doctor,' Salter said, rolling forwards. 'Everything has its price. And everyone.'

The Doctor shook his head. 'No,' he said firmly. 'Not everyone.'

Salter laughed. 'You're above such things, are you? Lucky you. The rest of us live in the real world.'

'But you put money into building the new terminal – why fill it with bombs?'

'Insurance,' Salter answered. 'Insurance is a way of preparing yourself for an unknown future. Everything in life's a gamble, one way or another.'

'But it's gambling that got you into trouble in the first place, am I right? Cards and the tables, bigger and bigger losses…?'

Salter shrugged. 'It's not an original story,' he confessed, 'but I doubt it's been done on this scale many times.'

'You owed Uncle so much that you needed to sabotage your own building?' The Doctor's tone made it clear how appalled he was.

'It was meant to be a win-win. Uncle would get his status back, and I would clear my debts,' explained Salter.

'And what about the death and destruction?' demanded the Doctor.

'You know the old saying about making omelettes…'

The Doctor's eyes narrowed. 'You just made your last mistake, Mr Salter. A hint of regret, a little compassion, that might have saved you, but you just don't care, do you? So now I will not be showing you any mercy.'

'What are you going to do?' laughed Salter, pointing a small but deadly handgun at the Doctor. 'Talk me into giving myself up?'

'Put down the weapon,' said the Doctor simply.

'Make me,' replied Salter, holding his gaze.

For a long moment there was silence.

'You see, you are powerless,' said Salter with satisfaction.

The Doctor shook his head. 'I don't think so. Do you?' This last question was directed at a point somewhere behind Salter. The old man spun around in his chair and found himself looking into the barrel of a Judoon blaster.

'For a creature of that size, my friend can move incredibly quietly,' said the Doctor.

'Justice should be swift,' the Judoon told the man in the wheelchair, 'but it does not have to be noisy!'

Salter started to laugh.

'What's so funny?' demanded the Judoon.

'You people. With your ridiculous ideas about fairness and justice.' He spun his chair to look back at the Doctor.

'You said you had no price. But you were lying.'

Salter flicked a switch on his chair, some kind of remote control, and a group of lights in the corner of the room came on to reveal a familiar blue box.

'Something you value quite a lot, I believe.'

The Doctor said nothing. There was something about the image that didn't ring true. The way it shimmered... 'That's just a hologram,' he realised.

'Of course. I have the real item hidden away. Along with all the other missing luggage. More insurance. Belt and braces. If anything happens to me, you will never know where. Believe me. If you want that thing back... you're going to have to let me escape.'

The Doctor shook his head gently. 'I know where the missing luggage is,' he said simply. Salter just stared at him, his mouth hanging open. The Judoon Commander reached down and removed the weapon from his hand and dropped it to the floor.

Salter rolled his chair backwards, looking up apprehensively at the Judoon.

'What's he going to do with me?' he stammered, glancing round to address the Doctor.

The Doctor shrugged. 'That's up to him.'

The Judoon took a step forward. 'Your bombs killed seven Judoon,' he told Salter. 'Justice must be swift.'

He raised his blaster and extended his arm. 'But there must be due process.'

He lowered his aim and vaporised Salter's gun.

'Derek Salter, you are under arrest for crimes against the people of New Memphis and the Judoon,' the Judoon Commander told Salter formally. 'Anything you say can and will be recorded and may be used in a court of law.'

The Doctor grinned. 'In other words,' he added, 'you're nicked!'

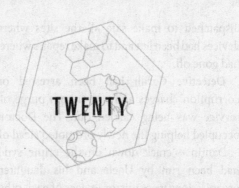

TWENTY

The Doctor and the Judoon Commander were sitting in a small café set in the foyer of one of the best hospitals in New Memphis.

The Doctor sipped at his coffee and looked around at the patients and visitors passing through the open foyer.

'There ought to be a little shop,' he murmured, a little disappointedly.

'There is one,' rumbled the Judoon, pointing towards a door leading to a side corridor. 'It's down there.'

The Doctor shot him a surprised look.

'I needed to buy a card for Nikki's father,' explained the Judoon.

For the last two days, the Doctor and the Judoon Commander had been busy aiding the city and the spaceport authorities recover from the mayhem of the previous forty-eight hours. Judoon troops had been dispatched to make safe all the sites where explosive devices had been left and to make repairs where explosions had gone off.

Detective Corilli had been arrested on multiple corruption charges and a thorough purge of the police service was being carried out. The Doctor had been occupied helping the newly promoted Head of Detectives – Dantin – crack down on the crime syndicates that had been run by Uncle and his daughter. The two organisations were mirror images of each other, and both were dependent on the leadership of their respective crime lords. Unfortunately, both of them were dead.

Hope had not managed to take the Doctor's advice. At least not quickly enough. She had been found near to the spaceport, the second and final victim of the Invisible Assassin.

In the vacuum created by the disappearance of both Uncle and the Widow, the two criminal operations were in considerable disarray. The police were able to pick up and charge a number of people for crimes dating back many months, if not years. Overnight it was as if New Memphis had turned over a new leaf.

'It won't last,' Nikki had said with considerable cynicism for one so young. 'There will still be plenty of work for detectives like me and Dad.'

The Doctor and the Judoon Commander had exchanged a look of concern at Nikki's words; neither of them was sure how much work Conrad would be capable of for some time. He had survived the tunnel damage caused by the detonator, but not without cost. He had numerous broken bones and had suffered a lot of organ trauma. Although neither the Doctor nor the Judoon wanted to mention it to Nikki, his long-term prognosis was far from positive. That was one of the reasons that they were here now, in the hospital. The consultants working on Conrad wanted to bring Nikki up to date with their latest thinking, and she had asked her two friends to come with her.

The Doctor looked over at his Judoon friend. 'Won't Judoon High Command be expecting you and your ships back on patrol?' he asked.

'The fleet has already departed this sector,' replied the Judoon to the Doctor's surprise.

'They've gone without you?'

'I...' The Judoon hesitated, as if unable to think of the right word. 'I resigned,' he said finally.

The Doctor just stared at him. 'Resigned?'

The alien nodded. 'I've learnt a new way to achieve justice... There is much work that needs to be done here in New Memphis.'

'Well, yes, I can see that... I am sure Dantin would be happy to take you on.'

Before they could discuss the matter further, Nikki joined them.

'They say you can come in now,' she told them.

The life-support equipment was discreet rather than overwhelming, but the Doctor could see at a glance that Conrad was in pretty bad shape. He lay in a support bed with wires, sensors and tubes connected to various machines and monitors.

'He was very lucky,' Nikki confessed. 'If it hadn't have been for you two, he wouldn't be here at all.'

'And if I'd let you go back into that tunnel you would be in the same condition,' added the Judoon gently.

Nikki nodded, acknowledging the facts. 'Thank you,' she said simply.

The Doctor cleared his throat. 'So what will you do now, Nikki?'

The girl shrugged. 'I guess I'll carry on the Detective Agency as best I can until Dad is well enough to come back to work.'

'That could be months,' the Doctor pointed out.

'Maybe you could stick around a little longer and help me out?' she asked with a grin.

The Doctor shook his head. 'Me. A private detective? Sorry, Nikki, it's just not me. I'm a traveller; I've got travelling to do... Places to go, monsters to scare, that sort of thing... But I do know of a suitably qualified candidate if you're looking for some help with the Agency...'

The Doctor trailed off and looked over at the Judoon Commander.

'Him?' said Nikki.

'Me?' said the Judoon.

'Why not?' grinned the Doctor. 'Nikki needs some help at the Detective Agency; you want to stick around New Memphis and do some good – it's a perfect fit.'

The Judoon lowered his head, embarrassed at the recommendation.

'You realise I'd be the boss, right?' Nikki pointed out.

'Of course,' rumbled the Judoon.

'And we'd need to work on some of your people skills,' she grinned.

'Justice must be swift,' the Judoon reminded her.

'But it's not just about the rules, is it?' Nikki countered. 'It's about empathy, sympathy, understanding people. It has to be done with a little… humanity.'

The Judoon nodded. 'Or Judoonity,' he said, and started chuckling. 'Don't you agree, Doctor?'

They both turned to the Doctor but he was no longer there.

'Doctor?'

Nikki ran to the door and looked up and down the corridor outside but there was no sign of the Doctor.

The Judoon came up quietly behind her and gently placed a hand on her shoulder. 'I don't think he likes goodbyes.'

There was one goodbye that the Doctor did want to make. He made his way back to Terminal 13 to check on Jase Golightly. He found the General Manager in a much happier state of mind and improving physically as well.

The new facility was now open again (although there were still a number of outstanding repair jobs), the backlog of missing luggage was being dealt with and, for the first time in the troubled terminal's history, things were running smoothly.

'There's just one thing I don't understand,' Golightly said when the Doctor popped his head in to check on him.

'Only one?' joked the Doctor.

'How did you know where to find the missing luggage?'

The Doctor smiled. 'My blue box gives off a very particular energy signal. I knew I could find it. And I knew it'd be with the rest of the missing luggage. I just got our Judoon friends to scan for it. Job done!'

Golightly glanced at his watch. 'Sorry, Doctor. I don't mean to be rude, but I've got a media interview to give…'

'Don't worry about me,' replied the Doctor. 'I'm off now.'

The journalist Stacie Jorrez arrived and began setting up for the interview. The Doctor watched as Golightly started answering her questions.

'So is this really a story with a happy ending?' asked the pretty young woman as her camera-bot floated between herself and Golightly.

The lens on the bot swung around to focus on Jase, who smiled and answered in a relaxed fashion.

'Long-distance travel is always stressful, Stacie,' he admitted, 'but here at Elvis the King Spaceport, and particularly here in Terminal 13, we are dedicated to making the whole process as straightforward as possible. We're here to enhance your travelling experience…'

The Doctor smiled to himself. For better or worse, Terminal 13 was back in business. Personally he preferred a less public form of transport.

Nikki sat in her chair behind the desk at the Jupiter Detective Agency and watched as her new partner showed their client in.

Mrs Kellingham looked a little nervous as the massive alien figure pulled out a chair for her, but she hid it well.

She'd been brought up to treat all living creatures with respect and, as an experienced traveller, she was used to dealing with aliens. Nevertheless, she'd never been quite so close to anything as big as a Judoon before.

She sat in the seat, gingerly, and waited for the young girl to speak. Nikki pushed a small box across the desk towards the elderly lady.

'Please – open it,' she said, trying not to grin broadly.

With nervous fingers, Mrs Kellingham opened the box and gasped. Inside the box was her watch. Nikki felt her heart leap as she saw tears form in the eyes of the old lady. Mrs Kellingham lifted the watch out of the box and fixed it on her bony wrist.

'I can't begin to tell you how grateful I am…' she began, her voice quavering with emotion.

'It's my partner you should thank,' Nikki told her, nodding in the direction of the Judoon, who bowed his head modestly.

'You were the one who found my watch?'

'We worked the case together,' explained the Judoon. 'We knew that the watch wasn't at the thief's apartment, so we had to track down his fence.'

'A third party that trades in stolen goods,' explained Nikki quickly.

'And when we found the right fence, he was persuaded to give the watch back,' concluded the Judoon.

'My friend can be very persuasive,' added Nikki.

Mrs Kellingham smiled. 'I'm sure he can be,' she agreed. 'He's joined your Agency?'

Nikki nodded.

'Then you will need those new offices I was talking about before. I'll have my property manager contact you,' the old lady promised her.

Nikki was stunned. Finally things were looking up for the Jupiter Detective Agency.

'That's why we do this,' Nikki told the Judoon, after Mrs Kellingham had settled her bill and left.

'For the money?' rumbled the Judoon, and laughed his drain-clearer laugh.

'For the job satisfaction,' she said slapping his wrist playfully.

Nikki leant back in her chair and put her feet up.

'You know I think this new partnership is going to work out just fine.'

Inside the TARDIS, the Doctor was wandering around the six-sided console, adjusting various controls. He had enjoyed his time on New Memphis. It had reminded him of something that he should never have forgotten: that he should always look beyond the surface when dealing with alien races like the Judoon. He had made all sorts of assumptions about the Judoon Commander, and many of them had been wrong. He hoped the Judoon would enjoy his new life working with Nikki and her dad. He was lucky to have found such good people. For a moment, the Doctor stopped, deep in thought and memory. The TARDIS felt so empty without a travelling companion. With a heavy sigh, he pulled down a lever and set the TARDIS in flight.

The Doctor sat back on the padded seat and put his feet up on the edge of the console. No one else was around to tell him not to. He sighed again. One day, he would meet someone to share his travels with him – he always did eventually. He'd had a peculiar feeling for some time recently that change was coming, he was sure of it, he could feel something lurking in his near future, something big, terrible and yet inevitable…

The Doctor shook his head. No point moping about things that hadn't happened yet. The future – his future – was a blank book. He had no way of knowing what it held for him; what monsters he might fight, what evil he might encounter, what worlds he might see, but he did know one thing… it would be an adventure!

Somewhere in the immense nothingness of the Vortex, an impossible blue box went spinning on its way…

Acknowledgements

I am indebted to a number of people who have helped me in producing *Judgement of the Judoon*, and I'd like to take this opportunity to thank them all.

First of all thanks to Albert DePetrillo, Nicholas Payne and Caroline Newbury at BBC Books, who all do such a great job, not only on this book but across the *Doctor Who* range. Thanks in particular to Justin Richards for giving me the opportunity to contribute to the world of *Doctor Who* fiction once again, and a big thanks to Steve Tribe for his excellent and efficient editing!

I also need to thank my patient family – my wife Kerry and my children Cefn and Kassia – who have had to put up with me wandering around the house muttering Judoon catchphrases for months on end.

Thanks, of course, must also go to the guv'nor, Russell T Davies, for creating the wonderful Judoon in the first place, and to the design team at BBC Wales for their brilliant realisation on screen, which helped make this such a fun book to write. Thanks also to Terrance Dicks who made the Judoon's first appearance in print so memorable. It was an honour – and a challenge – to produce the Judoon's next appearance after two RTD scripts and a Terrance Dicks book!

Thanks, too, to David Tennant, whose energy, enthusiasm and dedication to the role has made the Tenth Doctor such a joy to write.

The biggest thanks of all to everyone at BBC Wales, who all work so hard to bring *Doctor Who* to our screens. For those of us who can count our time as *Doctor Who* fans in decades, the last few years have been an incredible time. The Doctor promised us an incredible journey, and he hasn't let us down. So my final thanks, if you'll excuse the strange timey-wimeyness of it all, is a thank you for the future of *Doctor Who*! Thanks, then, to Steven Moffat, Piers Wenger and, of course, Matt Smith and all the writers who are busy creating the Eleventh Doctor's first series of adventures even as you read this book... This really is just the beginning!

Also available from BBC Books
featuring the Doctor and Martha
as played by David Tennant and Freema Agyeman:

DOCTOR·WHO

The Story of Martha

by Dan Abnett

with David Roden, Steve Lockley & Paul Lewis,
Robert Shearman, and Simon Jowett

ISBN 978 1 846 07561 2

£6.99

For a year, while the Master ruled over Earth, Martha
Jones travelled the world telling people stories about
the Doctor. She told people of how the Doctor has
saved them before, and how he will save them again.

This is that story. It tells of Martha's travels from
her arrival on Earth as the Toclafane attacked and
decimated the population through to her return to
Britain to face the Master. It tells how she spread the
word and told people about the Doctor. The story of
how she survived that terrible year.

But it's more than that. This is also a collection of the
stories she tells – the stories of adventures she had with
the Doctor that we haven't heard about before. The
stories that inspired and saved the world…

Also available from BBC Books
featuring the Doctor and Donna
as played by David Tennant and Catherine Tate:

DOCTOR·WHO

Beautiful Chaos
by Gary Russell
ISBN 978 1 846 07563 6
£6.99

Donna Noble is back home in London, catching
up with her family and generally giving them all
the gossip about her journeys. Her grandfather is
especially overjoyed – he's discovered a new star and
had it named after him. He takes the Doctor, as his
special guest, to the naming ceremony.

But the Doctor is suspicious about some of the other
changes he can see in Earth's heavens. Particularly
that bright star, right there. No, not that one, that one,
there, on the left…

The world's population is slowly being converted to a
new path, a new way of thinking. Something is coming
to Earth, an ancient force from the Dark Times.
Something powerful, angry, and all-consuming…

DOCTOR·WHO

The Slitheen Excursion

by Simon Guerrier
ISBN 978 1 846 07640 4
£6.99

1500BC – King Actaeus and his subjects live in mortal
fear of the awesome gods who have come to visit their
kingdom in ancient Greece. Except the Doctor, visiting
with university student June, knows they're not gods at
all. They're aliens.

For the aliens, it's the perfect holiday – they get to tour
the sights of a primitive planet and even take part in
local customs. Like gladiatorial games, or hunting
down and killing humans who won't be missed.

With June's enthusiastic help, the Doctor soon meets
the travel agents behind this deadly package holiday
company – his old enemies the Slitheen. But can
he bring the Slitheen excursion to an end without
endangering more lives? And how are events in ancient
Greece linked to a modern-day alien plot to destroy
what's left of the Parthenon?